SPINNER

and the
Wrath of the Mandrill

RELEASES BY LOOSE MOOSE PUBLISHING:

DAN DRAŽEN MAZUR

SPINNER
and the
Wrath of the Mandrill

LOOSE MOOSE PUBLISHING

ISBN 9780999752975
Printed in United States of America

Dedication

To all people of the United States who voted for Dwight Eisenhower, twice.

Acknowledgment

This, the second installment of Spinner's adventures, was written thanks to continuous support of Ranko Igrić and Pearl Savage.

Norma Mazur and Mark Wenden helped clean up the text, and the latter is to be thanked or condemned for the upcoming

Spinner - All or Nothing.

Finally, Robert Edwards stayed on board to design the book's interior. He also created the book's cover, and if it doesn't get everyone's attention, nothing else will.

CONTENTS

PART 1: FREE FALL

PART 2: DAMAGE CONTROL

PART 3: HAPPY ENDING

PART 1: FREE FALL

1

AARON and GARY

My name is Spinner, and my game is revenge. My first reaction and instinct told me that the idea was bad, crazy, dangerous, stupid, and what have you. Then I changed my mind and unfortunately decided to go ahead. In the aftermath it turned out that my initial feelings were right. Lately, my wishy-washy behavior seems to be present more than ever before. As I got involved in bigger things, they destabilized and made me even more irrational. I was aware of it, but I couldn't fight it. Apparently, I am not good at handling big things.

Take Charlie, for example. My alter ego, imaginary friend, if you like. He is not real, and I know it. Everybody has that other, little inner-self, interfering with one's decision making – advising, suggesting, interrupting, pushing. Not everyone wants to admit it, and not everyone has the guts to formulate it so clearly – even giving it a name, but we all have it, more or less. I wound up having it more. Charlie is ever present in me, residing in my mind and talking to me. He is friendly, caring; he gives me advice, influences my life. He can't read my thoughts, so I have to talk when I want him to hear me. I do that only when nobody else is present, because people are judgmental, and before you know it, they slap a label on you: 'crazy.' Once I was talking to Charlie in the presence of a hospital nurse and wound up in a straitjacket. You don't want to know.

Me getting bored and the fact that I just couldn't get rid of the anger accumulating in me worked on Charlie's behalf and helped him convince me. He took advantage of my condition and began persuading me that kidnapping Elizabeth, Mr. Laos' daughter, was a good idea, because it would give me something to do, and alleviate my anger. He was right about that. Mr. Laos is a billionaire who used me, crossed me twice, and made me feel like a fool in front of others. He awarded me a total of $600,000, but apparently that wasn't good enough to wash off the humiliation I felt for being naïve. I just couldn't get rid of the bitter taste the events left in me, and I tried not to think about what happened. I knew I should let it go and enjoy my easy money – but I couldn't. The guy was essentially a decent person, and this only increased my anger. Charlie knew all this and kept bugging me that something should be done about it.

Retaliation. Revenge. Payback. Making a fool of Mr. Laos. Let's use his daughter whom he loved very much. Do no real harm, only scare them, have him pay for making an idiot out of me. Finish with good laughter. This was the general idea.

I ended becoming sold on Charlie's proposal. He reiterated its sole purpose was to teach Mr. Laos a lesson about what one should expect when messing with me. However, from a 20-20 hindsight perspective, I have to admit that this was a terrible mistake.

I could blame Charlie for this, but he was only partially responsible. Ultimately, it was I who accepted his arguments and agreed to proceed with this bad decision. After all, Charlie was only my own, aggressive inner self, unable to achieve anything on his own. But he knew how to push the right buttons in me. He kept fueling my low self-esteem and took advantage of my self-imposed compulsion to retaliate for the embarrassment Mr. Laos caused me.

"You can do it, Spinner," Charlie kept nudging me, sensing my softening to his idea. "You know people, you have money, you can organize this and have some fun in the process."

This was easier said than done. I was a small caliber criminal, and kidnapping had never been on my agenda before. On the other hand, I had money and I was getting bored doing nothing.

So, I started thinking 'what if…' Logistically, there were major obstacles. If those could be resolved, number of various details would also have to be considered, predicted, addressed and worked out. Little by little, I was thinking about it more and more. I couldn't sleep well and gradually I became obsessed with the idea. It gave me indeed something to do – it made me feel useful again. It would give me a goal and keep me from remaining idle. It was like having a purpose in life again. I would no longer be the couch potato my girlfriend, Petra, accused me of becoming.

First and foremost, she was absolutely not to be involved. We lived together but were quite different people. In my eyes she was pure and innocent, a bit cold but very passionate for animals. On the other hand, I was less pure, less innocent and cared less for the animals. Petra's resume had no dark spots like mine. She worked for the City of Ceilings police department in a capacity that even today is not clear to me. For some reason I never asked her details about her job. Surely, she wouldn't approve of the plan and would try to talk me out of it.

I announced to Petra my plan to visit my mother and ailing grandmother, who were living in the Chicago area. Of course, this visit would not take place at all, but would excuse me for not being at home during the operation. Petra bought my lies and commented that it was about time to move my 'lazy ass' and do something proper. I was feeling guilty for lying to her, but Charlie put me at ease, stating that what we were about to do would not look very good on Petra's resume. In other words, my lying was justified.

I knew this was no one-man operation and I would have to involve accomplices. The action was to take place on Duke of Prunes Island, at the government's shady animal diseases study facility. They had an even more questionable secret experimental lab there involving humans, backed by Elizabeth's father. I knew the Island was well guarded and hard to approach. The timing of the operation had to be synchronized to coincide with Elizabeth's presence on the Island, and it was my understanding that she was seldom there. I knew some people who might be of help, namely Walter and Cho-Hu. Not exactly my friends, they were Mr. Laos' people but knew the Island well. In the past they had been pretty fair to me, and I hoped they could be useful in providing me the information I needed. They were also loyal to their boss, so I better be careful getting information from them, without raising suspicion that I was preparing something menacing. This wasn't easy, but at the end I thought I'd done a pretty good job in extracting the information I wanted, without alerting them of the plot and upcoming raid.

I also carefully renewed my association with Mrs. Miller, or the Spider-Witch, as Charlie called her. She was the mother of my car-mechanic friend Joe, who sheltered Petra and me when we thought our lives were in jeopardy. A strange lady, she tried to use me against Mr. Laos, whom she knew and disliked. I haven't seen her for some time now. When I contacted her again through Joe, I learned that she continued to hold grudges against Mr. Laos, even though he never pressed charges against her and swore that he never stole the spider anti-venom invention from her, nor sold it to the Australians. When I revealed to her a plan to kidnap his daughter, she agreed to participate, especially after I told her that the action would not harm Elizabeth but was designed only to scare Mr. Laos and make him think that he would have to pay a big ransom. She agreed to hide Elizabeth in her basement, which until then I didn't even know existed. I went to inspect it and found it to be a creepy looking place, dark, damp and full of spider webs. I suffer from mild arachnophobia and got out of the basement as fast as I could.

I also contacted some of my old friends who belonged to the American underworld and at the end hired two guys, Stan and Aaron, to help me execute the plan.

"You need to divert attention away from what you'll be doing, Spinner," Charlie suggested.

True. Aaron connected me to a radical animal rights group called 3ACS – pronounced 'three aces' – which stood for the American Anti Animal-Cruelty Society. They operated on the margins of the law, sometimes using questionable tactics to achieve their goals and make their point of view. They would distort the real reason for our presence on the Island. They would attempt to free the lab animals held there, to make their point: opposing the use of animals for experiments. They were willing to create a diversion and cause confusion, masking the primary reason for invading the Island – to kidnap Elizabeth.

Their leader, Gary, was a scary looking individual: I bet behind his back he was called a Scarface, because of visible scar decorating the entire left side of his face. He agreed to purchase all equipment needed for the operation with money I gave them. His group already planned to visit the Duke of Prunes Island anyway, but for various reasons this had never materialized. However, they had already worked out detailed plan to execute the operation and gathered much information about the Island's security, landscape and building configuration. This greatly reduced the amount of work for me.

All that was needed was a signal that Elizabeth was on the Island. Two weeks later I thought we were ready, but still no word.

"Take it easy, Charlie," I said loudly when there was nobody around to hear me, "be patient, don't push me."

"Festina lente, huh?" Charlie answered, forcing me to check what the hell that meant. He surprised me at times by saying something unfamiliar, peculiar. This was odd. I knew that it was me actually saying it. The strange thing was that I wasn't always aware I knew the things he would sometimes say. This puzzled me.

Petra became suspicious when I couldn't tell her the exact date when I would take off to visit my family. This made me nervous and I came up with some excuses, sounding so ridiculous that she actually believed them.

I spent days waiting for the signal and going over every detail I could think of. I thought everything was in place and that the plan was good, and that nothing could go wrong.

Finally, Cho-Hu called. Elizabeth had arrived on the Island and there were indications she would spend at least a few days there.

This was good, and I let Gary and my people know that we were good to go. Gary needed one day to assemble his crew, and the second night we would take off.

Petra was at work and I called her letting her know that I was leaving. We had lunch together. I kissed her and left, pretending to take off for Illinois. In fact, I met with Stan and Aaron, and three of us went to join Gary and his crew. His guys, seven of them, looked like professional criminals and not animal right activists. This was good. Hopefully.

I was excited, hoping nothing would go wrong, encouraged by Charlie's positive predictions.

It was an hour after midnight when we embarked on three inflatable rubber boats and pushed off the shore. I couldn't see anything, but Gary said I shouldn't worry about their navigation. After about an hour he said we were approaching the Island. He spoke into his walkie-talkie, instructing everybody to shut down the motors. The three rubber boat invaders continued in silence, and we were all quietly paddling. About 15 minutes later, we hit the shore of Duke of Prunes.

At that moment I somehow began regretting what I was trying to do, but of course it was too late.

2

RUDY and FIRE

Our three rubber boats were almost simultaneously stranded on shore, and we pulled them halfway out of the water. We were away from the buildings, but I could see them thanks to the yellow lights coming from bulbs mounted above their entrances. Clouds covered the moon and stars making the night pitch dark. All I could see were the silhouettes of people around me, and those poorly lit buildings in the distance.

"Put on the masks," Gary whispered, and we pulled over our heads the black ski masks each of us carried. The air was chilly, and it felt good having a mask covering and warming up my cold skin.

"We wait now," Gary continued. "I signaled Rudy that we're here."

Rudy? I'd never mentioned his name before. He was a snitch who worked on the Island as a grounds maintenance person but was also a member of 3ACS. During our prep time Gary told me about him. Rudy was to make our mission easier, even possible, as he was supposed to cut off the Island's electric power and guide us around the terrain in the darkness.

I was told that the security systems on Duke of Prunes were old, not updated much since the animal research center on the Island was established back in the 1950s. They included a motion detector system around the buildings that would turn on flood lights if movement was detected. That's why Gary wanted us to stay put and away from the buildings. There were also emergency power generators ready to kick in automatically in case of an electric power outage.

If all went as planned, we shouldn't worry about their security systems, Gary told me. Rudy was supposed to cut off not only the main power supply, but the emergency system as well, which should make it possible to complete the mission undetected.

What I didn't know at the time was that Rudy was also directed to start a small fire in the vicinity of the restaurant, or cantina, as they called it. This was to direct everyone's attention there and allow us to get to where we were going undetected. This was a double diversion that should cause confusion. It would help us capture Elizabeth, gag her, take back to our boats, and sail away prior to anyone noticing what was actually going on.

We were lying on our stomachs nervously observing the buildings. A few minutes later the lights went out. Now in total darkness we remained motionless in our positions, waiting for Rudy. The clouds thinned, and we could see a little better, thanks to stars peeking out between the clouds. My eyes adjusted to the darkness, and I could better see the shapes of my comrades, the buildings and trees in the distance.

After a few more minutes of waiting, I saw a small flame coming out of the restaurant. This was Rudy's doing, and we waited for him to show up and take us to the warehouse where they housed the lab animals. Their release would cause further distraction. Then Rudy would take me and my buddies to the building where Elizabeth was supposed to be sleeping.

The restaurant flames grew bigger and I saw the silhouette of a man running toward us. He had a flashlight and obviously knew exactly where we were. He had barely arrived when a loud and strong explosion shook the Island and us with it. I saw the structure literally exploding and pieces of debris illuminated by shooting flames high in the air.

"Gary?" Rudy inquired, unable to distinguish between the masked people laying on the ground, and ignoring the explosions coming from the restaurant.

"Here," Gary said loudly and moved his hand, making sure Rudy could see where his voice was coming from. "Jesus, Rudy," Gary continued, "are you gonna blow up the whole damn Island?"

"I don't know what's happening," Rudy answered and hit the ground next to Gary. "They must have stored explosives there, or something."

The electricity was out, but thanks to the light the fire produced we saw people running and yelling around the burning structure. Then I heard the loud sound of a siren, powerful enough to wake up everyone on the Island.

"Damn it, Rudy, you were supposed to cut off all the electricity. Didn't you?" Gary shouted.

"I've done my job, dumbass," Rudy answered. "What you're hearing is a manually operated air raid siren." He sounded a bit sarcastic and continued: "Follow me."

And without waiting a second longer he got up and began running away from the burning building, toward the labs behind it.

I'd been on this Island before and was somewhat familiar with the landscape and building locations. I remembered that behind the cantina, now in flames, were three or more buildings located toward the Island's middle section.

The plan was that Rudy would take Gary and his crew to the warehouse housing the lab animals and unlock the entrance. Gary and his people would enter and cut the chain link on the animal cages, letting some of them loose. The deal was only to set free a few dogs and cats, enough to make a statement, and cause an additional diversion. Gary's crew carried small but powerful wire cutters, and Rudy was supposed to leave the heavy-duty ones inside the building.

Rudy was then to take Stan, Aaron and me down to the building where I used to be imprisoned. That building also had private rooms for workers and guests. Elizabeth had her own suite there. The hope was that due to the commotion caused by the escaped animals we would bring Elizabeth back to our boats undetected. But now the fire and explosions at the restaurant made me doubt the whole thing.

I hadn't planned for this, and I didn't like it. Too much noise, too much confusion.

First, the fire and explosions at the cantina were disturbing. It seemed to be getting out of hand, and maybe people were hurt or died, which was a major concern for me. I didn't want that. This would also put all of us in big trouble. This was not supposed to happen; nobody was supposed to be hurt in the prank. Or, God forbid, perish.

There were several more explosions, and I was surprised that only a few people were seen running around. I had expected that everybody would flock around the cantina to see what the hell was happening. I began regretting the whole mission, but it was too late to abort it. I even hoped that Elizabeth might also be amongst those who left their room and had gone to see what was happening. If that was the case, the kidnapping mission would be unsuccessful – which at that point would be my favorite outcome.

In only a few more minutes I found out even these worries were nothing in comparison to what was really going to happen.

We arrived at the building. Rudy apparently knew the code and unlocked the building's entrance. We all entered.

"Gary, you guys do your job here, and you and your guys follow me," Rudy said pointing his flashlight at me.

Gary and his crew silently left, while Rudy, Aaron, Stan and I kept running through the building toward the exit on the other side.

Stan and Aaron ran close to me. They knew what their job was.

Four of us exited the building and Rudy continued running toward the next building. Arriving, he immediately began fiddling with its locking mechanism.

"We are here," Rudy said to me.

What? "Wait!" I yelled, suddenly realizing that something was wrong. If my memory didn't fail me, I remembered the first time I was on the Island, we passed through two buildings after exiting the cantina, and before reaching the building where we were supposed to go. It was Walter who was our guide then. I remembered seeing the letter 'W' on the first building, and Walter telling us that the lab animals were housed there. The next building was a highly restricted area, 'WAT,' where they kept animals used in genetic experimentation. I remembered seeing several severely deformed animals there, and others that could be categorized as monsters. Walter made a comment then that the tenants there were not harmful – they just looked a bit freaky.

Since we passed through only one building before reaching our target destination, I became suspicious that Rudy had left Gary in the 'WAT' building and not 'W.' I hoped I was wrong – they better not be releasing genetically modified animals.

"What, what is it?" Rudy asked and stopped working on the lock.

"Are you sure you left Gary in the right building?" I asked nervously.

Rudy paused for a second, and said: "What do you mean?" He paused for another second and shouted: "Shit! You're right, we better go stop them!"

And without waiting he turned around and ran toward the building where we'd left Gary and his crew.

I had no flashlight, so I could only see where Rudy and Stan were pointing theirs. One of them had a shaky light on the building door, and I saw two shadowy creatures running out. I could not even guess what they were. I couldn't see well, but just about everything I saw looked like a monster to me. The hair on my back rose, and my body was hit with an instant adrenaline infusion. Fear flooded me. I didn't know what to do, or where to go. I just froze for a moment, not knowing what the best move on my part would be.

Then I heard horrible human screaming coming out of that building. Fear overpowered me, and I turned and started backing off from the building's entrance. I saw a large silhouette gaining on me.

Stan or Aaron must have shined their flashlight toward me, and I saw a huge dog, whose skull looked enlarged and deformed, rapidly approaching. His mouth was open, and I saw his sharp canines and dripping saliva. The dog was an enormous Irish Wolfhound. His appearance put me into sheer panic. I saw another creature running after the dog, and when it came closer to me, I realized it was Walter, the guy I knew – Mr. Laos' man.

I had no time to process or reason what was happening. The dog was getting closer, and I thought this was the end of me. Charlie, my alter ego pal, also seemed to be petrified because he was not saying a word.

The animal ran right up on me, and I instinctively squeezed my hands into fists, and extended them to keep the beast away. The dog almost hit me but stopped right in front of me, causing dust to rise a few feet in the air.

At that moment I heard a voice: "Take me to your boat if you want to live!"

This was shouted in an almost unrecognizable human voice. I thought I had completely lost my mind, because it wasn't Walter who yelled this, but the Irish Wolfhound.

3

ALEX and REX

Soon enough I found out that the dog, or should I say the Irish Wolfhound creature, had three names. One was Alex. Another one was Olcan, and on the Island he was listed as FA1903.11. He wasn't a genetically modified animal, rather he was, as they called it, a fanimal. Fanimal was the term used for living organism that was the product of fusion between two or more different species. When I asked exactly what kind of fusion they were talking about, the answer was 'all kinds.' Many types of fusion were allegedly going on at the Duke of Prunes secret labs. I decided to call it a hybrid. Charlie later insisted that the term 'fusion' was more appropriate than 'hybrid.' Oh well.

The dog remembered living in a luxurious house owned by an old, wealthy Irish widow who bought him after her husband died. She named her dog Olcan, after an early Irish saint. She had him only a year or so before dying rather suddenly – after being diagnosed with an aggressive brain cancer. Her house, money, personal possessions and the wolfhound went to her niece who was the only family the old lady had. Her niece took the house, money and possessions, but dropped the dog off at an animal shelter. Big dogs were not easy prospects for adoption, and to avoid euthanizing too many excess dogs, the shelter would sell some surplus animals to labs, educational institutions and research facilities, for medical studies and experimentation. This transaction brought Olcan to Duke of Prunes.

Alex was a middle-aged construction worker who wore a helmet when the accident occurred. His body ended completely pancaked when a heavy load of galvanized steel pipe he was preparing for shipping fell on him. The accident left the upper portion of his head and brain nearly entirely intact. His driver's license indicated that he was an organ donor. This is how his brain wound up on the Duke of Prunes.

FA1903.11 was the result of transplanting, implanting and connecting Alex's brain to Olcan's, resulting in a grotesquely enlarged dog's head. The outcome was that the dog's autonomic nervous system was left undamaged and working well and adding a person's brain to it allowed it to talk and reason – made it human. Alex's brain was even able to access Olcan's memories.

Several fanimals on the Island were combination of human brains and animal bodies, but they were treated like any other research animal and kept together with other genetically modified experimental oddities. FA1903.11 talked, pleaded and demanded that he should be considered human and not an animal. His requests for transfer were denied. The current stage of the experiments on fanimals was focused on figuring out how to prevent organ rejection when different species were fused. FA1903.11 was tested, observed and given several substances in attempt to find the cure for organ rejection, but success was limited. He was told that unfortunately his days were numbered, and it would be for the best that he be kept together with other species of similar appearance – he looked like a dog and placing him with humans would only cause confusion and draw unnecessary attention.

I learned all this from that poor creature who patiently answered my questions and informed me about all this during our sailing from Duke of Prunes to the mainland. We were accompanied by Walter. The Irish Wolfhound didn't miss his first opportunity to escape from the hellish Island and didn't want to take any chances with Walter.

"You are going with us!" he said in his, difficult to understand dog's voice, and also let out a clear warning growl which convinced Walter to just nod and say, 'sure thing, of course.'

Poor Walter didn't know what was really going on. He couldn't believe his eyes when bumping into me on the Island during the animal rights activists raid. I kept to myself that the real target was Elizabeth, but he was looking at me suspiciously.

"You know, this is weird, man," he said, "what is your role in all this, anyway?"

I pretended not to hear the question, although I knew this was only postponing the inevitable, and sooner or later I would have to explain myself, not only to Walter, but to everyone else as well. Walter kept saying that what the activists did could have catastrophic consequences, because all kinds of 'stuff' were in that building. However, he refused to elaborate and give more details.

The explosions destroying the cantina was of especial concern to Walter, and he speculated that likely someone was killed or wounded in that event.

To state that being reminded of all of this was greatly disturbing for me would be a gross understatement. Whatever happened was a consequence of my stupidity. It completely sidetracked my mission which was idiotic anyway. It resulted in a disaster, for which I held myself utterly responsible.

My anxiety peaked thinking about all this. I was trying to justify and ease a bit of my own sense of responsibility, and more and more started to blame Charlie for the tragedy, at least partially. It was he who had talked me into this in the first place. It was his initial idea –

kidnapping Elizabeth! Totally stupid.

When we reached Mrs. Miller's house it was already dawn. As we came closer, we could hear wild barking coming from inside.

"There is a powerful dog in this house, a male," FA1903.11 said, "and he will attack me if he could. He will not obey his owner's commands."

"And you know all this only by sniffing the air here?" I asked.

The dog nodded: "You wouldn't believe how much information I can get from smelling and sniffing my surroundings. I can detect very tiny and weak odors with ease. Strong stenches could destroy my receptacles and harm me, if I didn't have a way to automatically filter them down to a level safe for my sensitive olfactory system."

We approached the house and heard Mrs. Miller's voice trying to shush Rex, her German Shepherd.

"So, what else can you smell?" I asked, intrigued.

"What, now?" he replied.

"Right now."

"For instance, I detect that last night there were four deer around the house. I can smell their fear. They were probably trying to avoid coyotes who were after them. There was also a squirrel and rabbits around, not to mention birds. And I can smell what you had for your last meal. You ate it in the company of a female who was ovulating. I presume it was your girlfriend. I can feel your high anxiety right now and smell that you are sweating and need to pee badly. Also…"

"All right, all right, you convinced me," I said, to stop him from saying something even more embarrassing to me.

We were in front of the house and I shouted: "Mrs. Miller, it's Spinner! Walter is with me. We also have a dog. Please keep your dog away and let us in."

Apparently, she had already put Rex away, because when the door opened, we saw her alone, sitting in her wheelchair, with her hair unruly and sticking out all over the place. She wore a long gray nightgown and had a deer hunting rifle with scope resting on her lap.

"Why do you have a dog? Where is Elizabeth? What is this person doing here?" Mrs. Miller fired her questions, raised her hand with the rifle in it, and pointed it toward Walter.

"Don't shoot me! Don't shoot me, please," Walter pleaded, raising his own arms as if he could protect his body from bullets. He rushed to remind her: "I am Walter, we met before."

"I remember, I remember. Ain't gonna shoot you, don't worry," she mumbled, and I quickly added: "Long story, Mrs. Miller. I will explain everything; can you for now just take us to the basement?"

"What about the dog?" she asked. "Him too?"

"Yes, ma'am," FA1903.11 said, and I couldn't help but laugh seeing the surprised expression on her face.

"What? Who said this?" she looked at the dog suspiciously. "You can talk?"

"I can talk. Please keep your German Shepherd away from me, because he wants to kill me."

"Right," she said, accepting the talking dog surprisingly easy, and turned her wheelchair to make room for us to enter.

"Anyway, what's your name?" she asked the dog.

"Alex."

"Right," she repeated and concluded: "What the hell is this world coming to?"

19

4

BASEMENT and TV

"Follow me," Mrs. Miller said, turning right at the corridor of the house, with Walter, Alex and me closely behind. Rex's barking from the other side of the hall did not stop. "I don't know what's got into him – I've never heard him barking like this."

"He senses I'm no ordinary dog," Alex explained. "He wants to protect you. And he is pissed he can't be with you to do his job."

"Right. He's great dog," Mrs. Miller concluded. She opened the last door in the corridor and turned the light switch on. The room was small – a spare bedroom. The twin bed in the room seemed to have been moved aside from its usual place and part of the carpet underneath was flipped over, exposing a trapdoor in the hardwood floor. With the bed and carpet in their original locations, it would be impossible to notice a hidden entrance to the basement.

Mrs. Miller got up from her wheelchair, leaving her rifle in the wheelchair seat, and inserted two fingers into a small hole in the floor, lifting up the door. A wooden staircase leading down to the basement was visible.

Walter and I knew that despite being in a wheelchair most of the time, Mrs. Miller could walk, but this was news to Alex.

"You can walk?" he said, surprised.

"As you can see, you and I put together could make a regular walkie-talkie," she said.

"Ha-ha!" Walter laughed. He seemed to be the only one who found the joke funny.

Mrs. Miller headed downstairs, keeping one hand on the rail, and warned us to be careful. The stairs were steep, and we should watch our heads. She switched the light on, and we found ourselves in a small, partially finished basement.

The room had no windows. Since I'd checked the place out, somebody had done some cleaning and had prepared the room for Elizabeth. The paint on the wall was not touched, it was old and peeling in places, but the room was partitioned on one side with a large comforter stretched on a rope across the entire space, hiding the portion of the basement that must have been left untouched. No question, it was Mrs. Miller who had done some work there. She brought in spartan furnishings – a rustic looking bed, simple padded chair, and an old TV set on a table with shaky legs. Sufficient to make a person like Elizabeth uncomfortable enough to believe that she had really been kidnapped. Instead of her, now it looked like the three of us would share the damn place – Walter, me and the dog. I just couldn't get myself to see the Irish Wolfhound as a person yet, despite my conviction that the brain was the prevailing factor to making that determination.

Mrs. Miller was not adequately immaculate in cleaning the place, not to the degree that would satisfy my quest for an absence of spiders. I worried that there could be spiders still present in this basement. I can't stand spiders and knowing that Mrs. Miller had a huge living spider collection upstairs gave me the heebie-jeebies.

"So, why didn't you bring Elizabeth? What happened? I set this room up only for her, not for two men and a dog. No offense," Mrs. Miller said and shrugged her shoulders, looking at Alex.

"Elizabeth?" Walter was surprised. "What on Earth does Elizabeth have to do with all this, Spinner?"

It was time to confess and admit my role in this mess.

"It's all my fault Walter. I organized the whole thing with the idea to kidnap Elizabeth and teach Mr. Laos a lesson, because of what he did to me."

"What?" Walter said. "Are you crazy? He didn't do you any harm. And he paid you, didn't he?"

"He sure did. I know, this was supposed to be a practical joke. I would never hurt Elizabeth. I see now this was a crazy idea. I hired those wacko animal activists. Tried to use them as a distraction, but everything went south. They set fire to the cantina. They didn't expect the damn thing would explode. I sure didn't, either. Animals from the wrong building were set free and now we are stuck here with Alex."

"Thanks a lot," Alex said.

Mrs. Miller shook her head in disbelief.

"Can't you do anything right, Spinner? This isn't good. Why did you come here if your plan didn't work? What do you want to do?" she asked.

"I panicked. I didn't know where to go. Alex practically hijacked us. I will turn myself in, but I need a little time to figure out everything. I'd like to have more information. I will need a good lawyer."

"You bet. And how did you wind up in all this?" Mrs. Miller turned to Walter.

"Alex threatened me. I heard a siren and went to check what was going on. I saw Alex running free and I followed him and bumped right to Spinner."

"I smelled freedom and went crazy," Alex clarified. "I knew they had boats and saw a chance to at least die free, and not caged. I agreed to come here because I have nowhere to go. I am divorced, no children. What irony – I used to call my ex a 'bitch.' I bet she would get a kick out of seeing me like this."

"Pardon me, is there a restroom here?" I asked. I couldn't hold it in any longer.

"Behind that curtain. It's a chemical toilet. This room is set up for only one person, not two with a dog."

"You keep saying that. I wish you people would stop calling me a dog," Alex said.

"Right. I know, we tend to refer to things as they look, and not necessarily what they are, which is not always the same," Mrs. Miller said. "Instead of us seeing you as a human trapped in a dog's body, we still see you as a dog who talks. Sorry for this. It will take some time to adjust."

I went behind the curtain and sat on the toilet seat trying to urinate and making as little noise as possible. People in the room were talking loudly. This was good, less embarrassing for me.

"How come this room has no windows?" I heard Walter asking.

"The house came like that. Perhaps they used this place to make booze during prohibition."

Charlie, my not so wonderful inner self advisor, finally spoke. "I know you don't like me interrupting you, but I just want to let you know that your idea not to rush is good. Get informed about what happened and try to minimize the damage."

"Shut up, Charlie. All this is your fault," I said angrily but quietly, so people from the other side of the curtain would not hear me.

"I'm sorry. I really am. How could I know," Charlie continued, "that guy, what's his name, would burn the place down, and bring the crew to the wrong building? Nobody could predict that."

"Yes, I know, Charlie. Shut up now."

I stepped back into the furnished part of the basement.

"There is a faucet in that corner, but it doesn't work," Mrs. Miller said. "Sorry. Here, use these wet wipes to wash your hands."

"Thank you," I said.

23

"So, what's your plan, Spinner? How long are we going to be captive here?" Walter asked.

"We need to know exactly what happened. I bet this will be on the news. Let's turn the TV on."

"It's an old TV," Mrs. Miller said. "No cable connection down here. We can try the rabbit ears antenna. If that doesn't work, we can go upstairs."

Mrs. Miller turned on the TV. We had to wait a few minutes for the TV to warm up. I started flipping the channel knob only to get a snowy screen with no picture. Finally, manipulating the antenna, I was able to get a low-quality picture on one channel. I recognized the regular morning program on one of the network's channels. It took several minutes for the news to come up. The first segment was about some international crises. This was good – an indication that what happened on Duke of Prunes was not given high priority. I was very nervous, even hoping that what happened there might not be newsworthy. But that was only my wishful thinking because the newscaster's next piece was about exactly that.

"One person is reported dead and three more injured last night in an incident on Duke of Prunes Island, off the North Atlantic coast, on which the controversial Federal Animal Disorder Research Center is located. This happened when several individuals broke into the facility and released animals used for research. There was also an explosion, causing casualties. The injured victims were airlifted to the mainland hospital, and we will follow up on their condition. The FBI and CID agents are already on the Island conducting a joint investigation. Details about this incident are sketchy at this time. We will have more about this later in our broadcast."

We listened to this report in dead silence. I felt a knot forming in my guts and I became sick to my stomach. I sat on the chair, crushed. My hopes that nobody was seriously hurt had not come true. My biggest fears had materialized. I became painfully aware that what had happened would change my life entirely. From that moment on my future would take a totally new direction. I saw myself as a killer; although not directly, I was responsible for death of someone innocent, someone whom I didn't even know and who hadn't done anything to me to deserve it.

5

3ACS and MILITARY

The first one to break the silence was Alex. But he didn't talk – he was growling. His growl was downright scary, deep and although not loud, it sounded hostile and threatening. What the hell?

This behavior took all three of us by surprise. Before any of us could react, the dog stopped growling and switched to talking.

"Sorry," he said, "automatic reaction. Somebody is outside the house. People with dogs."

"Shit!" Mrs. Miller exclaimed. "I better check and see what's going on. You guys keep quiet here."

She began climbing the stairs and halfway up turned toward us and asked: "Do you have your cell phones?"

"I left mine with the 3ACS guys," I said.

"Mine is in my room on the Island," Walter added.

"Mine was smashed in my pocket in the accident," said Alex completing report.

"How did they figured out where you might be, so quickly," Mrs.

Miller continued. "How did you guys get here?"

"Taxi," Walter answered. "Had to pay extra for Alex."

"Damn it," she mumbled. "Maybe the driver heard the news, and this will be goodbye to our little party."

She reached the top of the stairs and dropped the trapdoor closing us in. I heard her straightening up the rug, covering the trapdoor and pulling the bed over it.

"Maybe it's nothing, only hunters," Walter said.

"You are such an optimist, Walter," I said, hoping he was right.

"Better than being a pessimist, like you," he said.

"I am only a realist. This might be over. If they find us here, you guys should say that you're here against your will."

"Who knows what she's going to tell them," Walter speculated.

"Quiet. She's back in the room above us," Alex warned us.

We could hear Rex barking.

"What the hell is she doing?" Walter wondered.

"She brought her dog to mix up my scent with his," Alex explained. "This should confuse the visiting dogs, if they bring them to the room above this basement."

We listened in silence to what was going on upstairs. Rex's barking stopped. Mrs. Miller perhaps left the room, as I couldn't hear anything else.

Alex, however, could.

"She is now talking through a closed door to people outside. There are two men with two dogs, both male Belgian Malinois, related to each other."

"Must be the police. My life is over," I said, ready to surrender.

"Hush," Alex whispered. "She is letting these people in. They are talking. She is taking them away from our side of the house. Rex is closed off in another room. He is quiet."

"Why would she let these people into the house?" Walter quietly asked.

"How should I know? Maybe they have a search warrant. Perhaps she told them that nobody else but her is here," I said.

"What about her son? Doesn't he live here with her?"

"He used to. Maybe he's away."

"There was nobody else in the house when we got here, other than her and the dog, trust me," said Alex.

I got a sudden urge to use the bathroom. It was my physical reaction to the situation. I excused myself and went behind the curtain again.

I suspected I would be hearing from Charlie after being alone behind the curtain – and I was right.

"If they find you here, say nothing," he started. "Otherwise you could incriminate yourself. Wait to get a lawyer. You have money to hire the best lawyers. You committed neither first nor second degree murder. You could get a relatively easy sentence."

"Yes, but I will again be ridiculed by everybody for my craziness. This time, somebody paid for my stupidity with their life. How do I get over that, Charlie?"

"You can't change the past, Spinner, but you can change the future. You are remorseful, you can turn your life around and become a better person."

"Whatever," I said, getting even more upset listening to his preaching.

I finished my business and joined Walter and Alex. The fanimal immediately updated me about the situation.

"The dogs detected both scents, mine and Rex's, but I don't believe their handlers could understand that. They will likely conclude the dogs are only sniffing out Rex."

Good thinking on Mrs. Miller's part! We quieted down awaiting our fate. Walter and I were on the bed with our legs hanging down over each side of it, with the backs of our heads resting on the headboard, while Alex was lying down on the floor next to my side.

The TV was still on, with the volume turned down, and I watched in silence as the hostess and her guest preparing a quick but yummy looking meal. I realized I was hungry.

This also triggered my thoughts about the immediate future.

So what if they find me? So what if Mrs. Miller decided to turn me in, and in return gets herself off the hook? She could tell them that I forced her to hide us and get it over with. If that didn't happen now, it would happen later anyway. No way out of it. Perhaps I should just turn myself in and end the agony. And even if I survived this round, it would be only temporary. How long could we stay in Mrs. Miller's basement? I still couldn't decide what I should do. I am usually pretty well organized. Having a plan makes me comfortable, and this chaotic uncertainty was killing me.

Alex raised his head and sniffed the air. "They are coming to the room above us, we should be very quiet."

I held my breath and heard some commotion above us. Unintelligible distant voices, steps, and dogs. Was I going to hear the trapdoor opening? Would Mrs. Miller give me up? The movement above lasted only a few seconds when Alex quietly said, "it looks like they're leaving."

Relief, if only temporary. I heard nothing more. I wished I was a dog. Alex gave me a unique opportunity and direct evidence of the amazing capability of their senses. This was fascinating.

"She's coming," Alex said, and I too heard activity above us again. It must have been Mrs. Miller pushing the bed aside and lifting the carpet. Indeed, the trapdoor opened, and she came down. She looked tired and out of breath. She sat in the only chair in the room and looked at me.

"Got rid of them," she said. "Spinner, you owe me one. I am now an accessory to whatever shit you are in."

"I know, I know, thank you."

"Who was it, the police?" Walter asked.

"Worse. It was the military police," she sighed. "Didn't expect military cops. They were looking for Spinner. And, the dog. Didn't say why. What the hell went on at that damn Island, Walter?"

Walter shook his head. "The military is behind all this, you know. You guys wouldn't believe what kind of research is going on there."

Oh yes, I believed it. We had living proof here – Alex, a talking dog with a human brain. Was there anything else that could top this?

Alex brought to our attention the TV.

"News – latest news," he said.

I looked at the TV screen and saw the news starting. Walter jumped from the bed and turned the TV volume up, and we caught the news almost from the beginning.

"… was committed by a radical animal activists' group known as 3ACS. One person died in the attack, three more were wounded, and are recovering in a hospital, with non-life-threatening injuries. All members of the 3ACS group who invaded the animal research facility are in custody and cooperating with the authorities. There is an intense search launched for two unaccounted for individuals and a dog. They are Spinner Walker, and Walter Nichosian, and here are their pictures. They are not suspects at this time but only persons of interest. If you see either of these two individuals please report them immediately to the local police, or FBI. The missing dog is a large Irish Wolfhound who was used in medical research and released by 3ACS. He looks similar to the one shown here. The public is warned not to approach the dog because he is contagious and could infect people coming in contact with him. The nature of the disease he might be spreading has not been disclosed. While there is no reason for panic, anyone who sees the dog should stay away and call 9-1-1 right away. When found, as a precaution and to ensure public safety, the dog will have to be destroyed."

6

SPIDER-WITCH and TRAPDOOR

"Jesus, you are contagious?" I nervously jumped from my bed and rushed to the other side, by Walter, and Mrs. Miller who stood next to him. This was my futile attempt to protect myself from Alex who kept resting on the floor by my side. "Why the hell didn't you let us know you were contagious?"

Mrs. Miller also became upset and stiff. "No-one told me you are infected, either. This sucks. I didn't plan to die. At least not yet."

Alex sat, taking a typical dog sitting position. He was large, and half his body showed above the bed. He shook his head.

"People, I swear I didn't know I was contagious. I was only given the medicine to prevent organ rejection. Damn it, Walter, what's going on?"

Walter appeared a bit calmer. "This is crazy. As far as I know, you're not contagious. I think I would know. I think they are bluffing."

"Why would they lie?"

"Think about it," Walter continued. "We have a talking dog here.

If he begins talking to people, they will freak out. This would cause an extreme sensation. Experiments like this one aren't exactly disclosed to the public. I think claiming that the dog is infected and should not be approached is just an effort to cover up the damage caused by his escape. They hope this will prevent the public figuring out that producing fanimals like Alex is part of the programs on Duke of Prunes."

"Fanimals?" Mrs. Miller said.

"Creatures fused from different species, like Alex is," Walter explained.

This sounded logical to me. Walter might be right. After all, we had been in close proximity to Alex for quite some time now and nobody showed signs of any illness – yet. Anyway, it almost didn't make any difference to me. I felt dead already.

Mrs. Miller seemed to share the same sentiment, because she also relaxed.

"I hope you're right, Walter," she said. "He didn't make me sick, and other than having a head like a potato, Alex looks like an ordinary dog. He doesn't even shed much."

"Irish Wolfhounds don't shed at all," Alex said. "I don't feel sick either. Maybe I'm not dying. Everybody seems to be lying. I don't feel any organ rejection. And I need to pee."

"You won't be going around the house lifting your legs left and right, and marking your territory, I hope," Mrs. Miller quickly said.

"Oh no, I think I can use the toilet. Somebody needs to lift the seat for me, please."

"I will," Walter said. He got up and pushed aside the comforter used as a room separator. Alex followed, and both disappeared behind the curtain.

I was processing what else I heard in the news. It was not good. They announced my name. They knew I started it. I was a person of interest. Petra must've heard it too. She knew I lied to her. She would probably kick me out of her house, and out of her life.

"You don't look good, Spinner," Mrs. Miller said, and I sensed a dash of sympathy in her voice. "I know things are bad, but they could be lot worse, believe me."

"You mean, in addition to my life being completely ruined, and me going to jail? Because of me, people died and were hurt, and all this due to my stupid practical joke that cost me almost a hundred grand, and that my girlfriend will likely want to have nothing to do with me? You're right, it's not that bad – I don't have a runny nose," I said bitterly.

"Nah, nah, you don't need to be sarcastic, Spinner. Don't forget, every cloud has a silver lining."

What the hell was that supposed to mean? Where was this sudden outburst of optimism coming from? I bit my tongue and said nothing, concluding that Mrs. Miller was only giving me a pep talk to bolster my morale, and cheer me up a bit. Rather than being snappish I should be thankful.

Walter came back while Alex remained behind the curtain.

Mrs. Miller turned practical. "Well, I think we should wait and stay put. We need to watch more news and see how things develop. This will give Spinner a chance to decide what to do. In the meantime, I have to feed you. I have pizza in my freezer. Alex, what about you?"

Alex had just come back from behind the curtain. "You mean, food? My digestive system and metabolism are that of a dog. Dog food would be fine, thank you."

"Good. I'll get you some of Rex's food. He gets diarrhea if he eats anything but dry dog food. I'll bring drinking water for everyone. Sorry, we don't serve alcohol."

She started climbing the stairs. "I will keep the trapdoor blocked, in case of more visitors."

"Thank you, Mrs. Miller," Walter said.

When she left, the conversation quieted down, giving me a chance to process what we heard on the latest news report. Still leery about Alex, I wondered if he could be infectious, and what kind of germs he might be passing on to us. I was not entirely sold on speculations that this information was a gimmick to prevent the public from realizing that a dog could talk. Most bothersome to me was that Petra probably knew I lied to her when I said that I was visiting my mother and grandmother in Illinois. She must have heard that I was a fugitive, and probably already blamed me for the death of the person on the Island. And rightfully so. It was likely she was the one who directed the authorities to check on Mrs. Miller's house for my possible whereabouts. She knew I had no other place to go.

Had I managed to completely ruin my life and future in one single night? You bet. And all this for a stupid prank? Check. Revenge? Absolutely. To scare Mr. Laos? Yep! What an idiot I was. I desperately needed an excuse and to find someone to blame – Charlie? Who else? I was reluctant to talk to him in front of other people, because I remembered well how they reacted when they heard me arguing with myself.

Walter jumped from the bed and turned the TV volume back on. "They have more news," he said.

I focused on the screen, which was showing a female newscaster:

"…interrupt our regular programing to bring you the latest news in connection to an incident that took place last night at Duke of Prunes Island. There are reports that the U.S. military sealed off the small coastal community of Sunolville, population 3,000, located on mainland across the Duke of Prunes. All access roads to the village are blocked. Communication lines – radio, telephone and internet signals coming out of there are scrambled, presumably by the military. The authorities issued a warning that all civilian traffic in or out of the village is suspended until further notice. A no-fly zone is proclaimed within a 20 miles radius around the village. Surrounding area residents seem to be rushing to leave the area and are trying to drive away, causing a traffic jam."

What the hell was happening? All this made me even more upset and I didn't think I could take much more. This was now turning into widespread disaster. This was the straw that broke the camel's back. I was that camel and came to my final decision. It was cowardly – I decided to surrender and put other people in charge of my destiny.

"Mrs. Miller!" I shouted. It looked like she hadn't heard me, so I climbed the stairs and began frantically banging on the trapdoor. I felt like something had possessed me, as I just wanted to get the hell out of there. This got a reaction from Rex and I heard him barking. Then I heard Mr. Miller's voice.

"Spinner, is that you screaming? What is it?"

"I've decided! I want to surrender. I've had enough. We've all had enough. Please open the door."

"What about me?" she sounded worried. "I'm gonna be in trouble too."

"Well, do you have a better idea? Tell me."

Silence.

"I know, ultimately there is no way out of this," I finally heard her voice through the door. "Give me ten minutes to think, and we will discuss this."

"There is nothing to discuss, Mrs. Miller," I said adamantly. "I want this uncertainty to be over."

"I know," she said. "Please, just give me a few minutes, Spinner. I think I deserve ten lousy minutes."

"All right," I said reluctantly. "Ten minutes, but no more."

Gee, I hoped the old woman wouldn't decide to keep us in her basement as prisoners. We should be able to break open the ceiling trapdoor by simply pushing on it, despite the bed blocking the door from above. Unless she blocked the trapdoor with additional weight. No, I hoped it wouldn't come to that.

"Don't be so sure that Spider-Witch won't keep you here," Charlie started, guessing my fears. "I know you think you can push the trapdoor open, but keep in mind Spider-Witch could put a bunch of containers with spiders on the bed, and tell you she will set them free, if there is an attempt to push the bed over. She knows how to keep you from trying to break out of the basement."

"Damn it, shut up, Charlie," I said. "You cooked all this up anyway. I shouldn't have listened to you. I'm sick of your advice. You only make things worse."

I saw Walter open his eyes wide. He knew I had no microchip called Charlie in my brain and must have concluded I went berserk.

"Whatever, man," he said. "Please just don't hurt us."

"Don't be ridiculous," I responded. "I am not crazy."

"What about me?" Alex asked. "They will shoot me the moment I show up."

Charlie continued talking to me. "Remember, I'm on your side, Spinner. I'm only trying to help. We are one and the same. I'm only giving you information you already have, but because you are upset you might not see it clearly at this moment."

"I know," I said. "This is all too much for me. If she tries to keep me here and doesn't open that door, I will explode. Spiders or not, I'm gonna open that damn door."

I heard commotion in the room above us. Moving the bed aside and opening the trapdoor. Mrs. Miller showed up on the stairs. All my anxiety was for nothing – thank God.

"Spinner, before you surrender, I think you might try one more thing," she said. "I called Mr. Laos and told him you were here, and what you plan to do."

"What?" I said in disbelief.

"I said nothing about your original plan with Elizabeth," she continued. "He said he would like to talk to you before you surrender. It is entirely up to you to take his suggestion or not. If I don't get back to him and let him know that you rejected his proposal, early tomorrow morning he will be sending a car to collect you. In the meantime, you can spend the night here, and tomorrow see what he has to say. If you accept, the meeting is on Duke of Prunes Island."

I was taken by surprise with this. What in the world did he want? I scratched my head.

"Don't take this offer," Charlie suggested. I wasn't sure. I was at the point to do just the opposite from what Charlie proposed and this time my curiosity and hope, that maybe, just maybe the man might have some kind of solution for me that would ease my situation – perhaps I shouldn't pass on that chance. Sorry, Charlie.

"I can't believe it. Did he say what he wanted?" I asked.

"He said this was entirely up to you, but he'd like to give you the news firsthand. He said, if you are interested, he has some good news and some bad news for you."

7

WALK and TALK

The early morning sky turned from pitch black to dark blue, growing lighter. Traces of orange and bloody-red clouds started peeking on the horizon in front of me. The sun quickly announced the dawn of a new day, coloring it purple, changing the Island shades from black to gray. We were gliding smoothly toward the dock, and I saw a person standing on the shore. Mr. Laos. He wore light colored clothing and a panama hat, apparently already waiting for us. The air was still and cold, and I would be shivering had I not worn the wind jacket Mrs. Miller let me borrow from her son's closet.

Mr. Laos showed no intention of helping secure the small boat that brought me there, but obviously Cho-Hu was used to handling the boat on his own. He stretched out his leg and prevented the boat hitting the stone quayside, and then jumped out on the dock, carrying the line which he skillfully wrapped around a rusty iron post.

It was Cho-Hu who came to Mrs. Miller's house to pick me up. The oversized black automobile had tinted windows, and we arrived at the harbor fast and without incidents. He pointed to a small fishing boat which would take us to Duke of Prunes. Cho-Hu was unusually reserved and wouldn't answer my questions, so most of our trip passed in silence. My imaginary friend Charlie was also quiet. I must have pissed him off by frequently criticizing his opinions and latest suggestion not to take Mr. Laos' invitation to meet.

While the boat was still mildly rocking, I stepped out on the shore. Mr. Laos approached.

"Great to see you, Mr. Spinner," he greeted me. I only nodded. I was in a dark mood. Maybe it was depression. Neither excited nor curios, I was only very tired. I'd spent another sleepless night anticipating this mysterious meeting, and the night before was the night of my stupid mistakes. The prospect of going to jail no longer seemed so bad. Why did I even agree to come back to the Island? I looked around. It was hard to believe I was there just hours earlier, with a bunch of rough guys, and we'd caused havoc. One person perished in fire; others were injured. I'd caused property damage and because of me a fanimal called Alex escaped. A dog with a human brain. And who knew what went on in Sunolville, that village across Duke of Prunes. No, whatever Mr. Laos wanted to tell me couldn't top that.

Mr. Laos realized that I wouldn't answer his greeting and he turned to Cho-Hu.

"Please wait here for us, Mr. Cho-Hu," he said. "Mr. Spinner and I will take a little walk around." And he extended his hand in the direction of the closest building. We started walking next to each other.

I devoted some attention to my surroundings. There were no people around, and the door of the building was wide open. The atmosphere was kind of eerie, but I couldn't pinpoint where exactly this feeling was coming from. Perhaps because this was the same building I'd passed through when Petra and I first came to the Island. Next to the door was a sign 'Registrations.' I remembered inside was a small waiting room, and behind a counter there had been a woman staring at computer monitors.

We entered the building and found ourselves in the same waiting room I remembered, only this time everything was empty, stripped down – computers, office desks, cabinets, and pictures – nothing was left. Evacuated, abandoned. Gee, I was thinking, how was this done in one single day?

I looked at Mr. Laos. "Please follow me," he said, and we went down the corridor and exited the building through a door on the back side. The next building was 'Cantina.' This was where Rudy, the 3ACS' mole on the Island, started distraction, what was supposedly to be a small fire. Everything went wrong from there. The fire took off, something exploded, a person lost her life, others were wounded. This recollection caused me a great discomfort. I expected Mr. Laos would show me the damage we caused, the location where injuries and death occurred. But he just kept walking through the building, and we exited from the back, the same quick way we'd passed through the first one. I noticed some minor fire damage and on the outside wall was a great black spot of smoke – probably where Rudy started a fire. However, I couldn't see the damage caused by the explosions I had witnessed at the time of our mission two nights ago. It was surprising that the interior of the building also appeared relatively intact, but completely evacuated. I remembered seeing things flying around when the building exploded. What happened?

Only a few tables and chairs were still there, but the tablecloths, utensils, plates and smaller items were not. There were no food trays, nor food visible behind the counter in the kitchen, and the pots and pans were also gone. The place appeared abandoned, just like the Registration building. I wondered again how it was possible to totally evacuate the building in such a short time.

Mr. Laos didn't talk, and walked away toward the next building, which was warehouse Nr. 1, where the lab animals were kept. This was where the 3ACS crew was supposed to release some animals, but instead wound up in the wrong building. I assumed the same pattern would repeat, and I was already prepared to encounter the evacuated structure, especially after noticing that the entrance door to that building was also wide open. I was right, inside was only an open space, dusty and with no animals, the cages were all removed and dismantled, and even the security cameras were missing – everything was gone.

Then there was the infamous, highly restricted WAT building from which Alex had escaped, after the 3ACS guys and Rudy, went in. Inside I saw only empty space, hollow, and uninhabited. What the hell happened? I was puzzled. One question kept coming to mind – how was it possible to evacuate everything and everybody in a single day, so fast, so thoroughly, and so efficiently? And why?

Like time and time before, Mr. Laos seemed to read my thoughts.

"Surprised, Mr. Spinner?"

"I sure as hell am," I said. "How did you vacate the Island in such short time?"

Mr. Laos didn't answer. We were outside. The sun was out, promising a gorgeous day, with a few white clouds decorating the blue sky. Pleasant air temperature – another ingredient to bring joy and happiness for being alive. Yeah, right, but not to me. With his left shoe Mr. Miller started drawing circles in the dirt, doodling. He was ready to talk. But he didn't.

"Well, what's the scoop?" I asked impatiently.

Mr. Laos smiled, put both his hands into his pants pockets, and finally opened his mouth.

"I believe Mrs. Miller told you about some good and some bad news. Here is the good news, Mr. Spinner. You'll be glad to hear that nobody died in your senseless action on this Island. Nobody was even hurt. You're not a murderer and won't be held responsible for anything of the kind. Now you can stop worrying about that part of your qualms."

He paused. Silence. I heard what he said but didn't quite get it. It simply didn't compute. Really? How? How come? What? Had I been fooled again? Was this another 'here we go again' moment? I should probably feel a sense of relief. The way he said it, I knew it was the truth. A part of me was telling me it maybe it was time to celebrate. But there was another part, hanging like a dark cloud over my head, a part reminding me that there was also the bad news ahead. This cloud wouldn't let me relax, feel the catharsis – nothing.

Of course, I deserved an explanation. I needed to hear more. I didn't have to wait long to get one.

"You asked how it was possible to evacuate the Island in one single day. You're right," Mr. Laos said. "That would be impossible."

I was puzzled. "What's going on here?"

Mr. Laos began walking toward the building where I was once held captive. I followed. The unpleasant memory of the event overwhelmed me, and I became even more uncomfortable. I forced myself into thinking how I was off the hook regarding my murder conviction, but it didn't help much. I knew there was more to come – let me hear the bad news.

"You see," Mr. Laos continued, approaching the building, "If you recall I promised your girlfriend, Miss Petra, that I would honor her pet peeve and make more humane treatment of animals one of my charitable causes. I checked into what it would take to improve the facilities here, on Duke of Prunes. The reports have shown that such a project would be costly. Very costly. Essentially, everything would have to be torn down and rebuilt from scratch. Everything we had here was old, obsolete, and not up to current standards. To bring it up to date it would cost just too much. And being located on an Island makes it very impractical and even more expensive. So, I proposed we should move the entire operation elsewhere and build a brand-new, modern facility. I have some property in Kansas that would be suitable for this. I offered to donate almost 1,000 acres of my land, and to invest 200 million start-up dollars as seed money. Need I say that the proposal backed with such a significant incentive wasn't turned down, and just about a month ago a temporary facility in Kansas became ready, enabling us to secretly move the operation there and we are now in the process of setting everything up for permanent use."

Wait, wait, wait! I was confused. I didn't quite get it. What about the raid on the Island, fire, explosions, animal escapes, people dying, people recovering in a hospital, TV reports, and all that? What the hell?

"Knowing you," Mr. Laos continued, "you will see this as bad news, Mr. Spinner, although it's not necessarily so. Mr. Spinner, loyalty is a trait that I value above other virtues, and too bad there is less and less of it existing in our modern world. I'm very careful who I associate myself with, and loyalty is very high on my list of requests. You, for example: loyalty is also one characteristic of your psychological profile. I like that. I'm telling you this to make it easier for you to understand what I'm going to say next. When you called Cho-Hu asking questions about Elizabeth, he immediately reported this to me. So, I knew that you were up to something even before I got a call from Mrs. Miller advising me that you planned to kidnap my daughter, in retaliation and as a lesson for the humiliation I allegedly brought to you."

This was dumbfounding. I felt like somebody hit me with a two-by-four. I was angry and above all, ashamed. Cho-Hu I could understand, but Mrs. Miller? Just about every time I encountered the man in front of me, he came out smelling like a rose, and I looked like a damn schmuck. Even the old Spider-Witch was now loyal to Mr. Laos? She, who I thought hated him?

"Mrs. Miller told you?" I said, astonished. "I don't understand. She doesn't even like you."

"She actually tolerates me," Mr. Laos said, laughing. "I talked to her to clear up her misunderstanding that I stole her antivenom for spider bites and sold it to the Australians. I believe she now trusts that I didn't do it. To seal the deal, I offered her a monetary compensation.

The amount was enough to put her, as you like to say it, in my pocket. So yes, she advised me of your little plot. I knew something like this could happen, because as you know I have created a very detailed psychological profile of you. It says that your sense of pride is significant, and the amount of money you earned in your dealings with me might not be sufficient to heal your wounded ego. I decided to teach you a little lesson that it was quite foolish to spend money on a questionable cause, depending too much on people you didn't know well enough, and planning an operation that carried such a high level of uncertainty, with a potential to turn into a disaster."

Yes, he was right, I was bitterly thinking. But, how? How did he pull it off? I had a ton of questions buzzing in my head. It was difficult to accept that I had been tricked again. I was dying to hear how he did it, and he immediately addressed the issue.

"Actually, it was easier than you probably think, to pull this off. It cost me a pretty penny, though. When I first learned about your plans, everything from the Island had already been moved to Kansas. I was able to use this as a stage for my lesson! I hired a motion picture production company and told them I wanted to make a movie that was to be produced and recorded as a documentary. The movie was about a disgruntled person who intended to kidnap a daughter from a wealthy family and demand ransom for her release. Sounds familiar? The whole shebang was to be shot only once, with several hidden cameras. They used several actors and actresses to act as Island personnel. Everything was staged! Fire and explosions were fake, and nobody died or was hurt during filming. I knew that you would need accomplices, and I set you up with Stan and Aaron. They were told to suggest hiring an animal rights group, as a distraction… Everything was staged, Mr. Spinner! They were all paid to participate in the movie. They knew that only you, although a main protagonist, was unaware that all this was a movie production. This was supposed to make it look more realistic."

I listened to this with my mouth open. I was flabbergasted. The old bastard had fooled me again. I thought cynically – by now I should already be used to it. But details, I couldn't think how did he manage the details?

"What about the damn TV news reports?" I wanted to know. "These people are real TV personalities, even celebrities – I watch them every day?"

"If you are willing to spend money, you can buy things like that. They were well paid to read my script about the disaster. They were told this was a part of a movie. It was recorded and incorporated into regular programming and played back on the only TV set you had access to. We had to make sure you couldn't have access to other TV channels and realize that nobody else was talking about Duke of Prunes. Mrs. Miller's basement was an ideal place for this. We made you believe there was reception on only one single channel."

I didn't know what to think. I was probably the most gullible person this guy ever met.

"What about Alex? Don't tell me the talking dog was also an actor."

"No, no, Alex is a real fanimal, and product of our research. He badly wanted to leave the Island and agreed to play the part of an escaped creature. He promised to be only a dog out there, and not let anybody know his true nature. Walter is his designated guard. Unfortunately, Alex is not well – we saw signs of organ rejection. The rest of his days he will spend with your girlfriend, Miss Petra, who agreed to play along. She was quite upset that you cooked up such a foolish and dangerous scheme."

Petra! I didn't know what would be worse: her believing that I was a murderer or a damn fool who fell in Mr. Laos' trap again. A trap that I dug myself.

"I'd like to go home. I must see Petra," I said.

"Afraid this is not possible, Mr. Spinner. You see, now you think you know all there is to know, and everything is over. Unfortunately, it's not. I need your help with a big problem and to prevent something really bad from happening."

I reacted on impulse.

"I don't believe a word you say and I'm not helping with anything. Can you imagine how I feel right now? I am not interested in dealing with you any further, Mr. Laos. I just want to go home."

"Mr. Spinner," Mr. Laos said with a very serious voice, "I can only imagine how you must feel. But there is another reason you were brought back to Duke of Prunes. Before turning me down you should listen to what I have to say. Let me clarify, it is not that I need help from you directly. It's not you who could help me in this, but your buddy, Charlie."

8

MOTHER and MONEY

I should have been surprised, but I wasn't. The man seemed to know everything about me, including having my secret inner advisor, Charlie. I wasn't even embarrassed any more. He could work with Charlie, my imaginary friend, and label me a lunatic – so what? In a sense I deserved it and I didn't feel completely normal anyway. I accepted the fact that I couldn't hide anything from this man.

"You don't seem surprised that I know about Charlie, Mr. Spinner," he said, and began walking back toward the dock with the fishing boat.

"I know, I should be, but I am not. You know everything about me and can't surprise me anymore," I said.

"It's time to go back to shore," Mr. Laos said and kept walking. "Yes, I do know quite a lot about you. You know that before I created your psychological makeup, I checked you out thoroughly. I learned a lot about you. There was a strong possibility that because of your genetic predisposition you might develop a strong alter ego. This you derived from your mother. I know she is a very religious woman. During your childhood you had some unpleasant clashes with her that were recorded in your school documents. Your mother carried a tremendous amount of guilt for having you out of wedlock. She spent a few years in Latvia hoping your father would marry her. You were born there, and when she couldn't establish a family with your father, she returned to the U.S. and immersed herself deeply in religion. She raised you by letting you know that Jesus taught her how to choose between right and wrong. She hoped that you would accept the words of Jesus. You resisted and called her crazy. You took her to be a very religious person bordering on being mentally disturbed."

"Please, leave my mother out of it," I said, trying to find words to defend my mother. I was still unsure how I felt about my mother, but I knew one thing – she wanted the best for me although in my view didn't always find the best methods to achieve that.

"I am just saying you inherited from your mother a predisposition to develop your own alter ego and if given the opportunity I predicted you would do so, and so you did."

"What do you want from Charlie, and why can't you get this directly from me?" I asked, still resisting to offer any assistance.

"You must have noticed that Charlie sometimes tells you things that he obviously knows, but you think you don't. This might puzzle you, because you are aware that he can't possess any knowledge outside your own experience. And yet, it happens. This is because we all have a photographic memory and remember just about everything we encounter in our life. Only a few individuals could consciously access those deep memories which are usually buried in the basement of our minds, and not readily available. Sometimes, under hypnosis we can access them. To the contrary, our alter egos can get to this information easily, without any problem. This is why I need Charlie's help, and not yours."

I became curious but was still unwilling to help.

"What exactly do you want from Charlie?"

"Well, the first time you came to this Island, when Walter took you through the WAT building, there was one particular metal cage near the entrance. On the front of the cage was a label, a mailing label, and I need to know the name on that label, and the address. I thought that perhaps Charlie would be able to dig this information out from your memory. I know you are very observant, and I believe you saw it."

I was still unwilling to help but became even more interested. I also knew Charlie was listening, but he remained silent.

"What is so important about it, and why do you need it?"

"It's a long story, Mr. Spinner," Mr. Laos sighed. "When we were moving to Kansas, this cage didn't make it to its destination. It disappeared, and I first assumed sloppiness was to blame. But I had to rule that out. We are still trying to figure out what and how it happened. We can only speculate about it. But, the address on that cage could be a lead that would help us recover it, and to do so is very important, Mr. Spinner, because if we don't recover this cage, very bad things could happen."

"Couldn't you get the address through the security camera recordings?"

"We tried but the cameras didn't help. They were positioned too far; they were old and with low resolution. We also hypnotized a few people, including Walter, who could have seen the label, but with no results. The person who was in charge of this cage is missing too."

"What was in that cage?"

"Initially, the monkey, but a few days before our move, the monkey was operated on and he became a fanimal."

This raised my curiosity level even higher. I signaled to Mr. Laos to go on.

"Mr. Spinner, I'll hide nothing from you, but you should let me know if you are willing to ask Charlie to retrieve that address."

I sighed. We were coming close to the dock and I stopped at a fair distance, so Cho-Hu wouldn't hear us.

"Charlie, can you hear me?" I said quietly.

"I hear you; I hear you," Charlie answered, but in a female voice. He was still pissed at me.

"C'mon Charlie, I'm not in the mood for games."

"I know," Charlie said, changing back to his regular voice. "You shouldn't act too fast on this one, Spinner. The guy needs information only we can provide. Maybe he should pay something for the favor."

Money. Charlie was thinking about money even in a situation like this. But he was right. Information was a commodity and had a value. And we had the info, and the old billionaire needed it. He should pay for it. Nevertheless, I felt quite uncomfortable spelling that out to him. Instead, I said, "Charlie wants to think about it. He isn't sure he can get this information and he wants some time."

"Good finesse, Spinner," Charlie praised me.

"There is no time Mr. Spinner," Mr. Laos said. "I'm amazed that the catastrophe hasn't start yet. It could happen any moment."

"How could one monkey be so dangerous?" I asked. "Are you trying to trick me again?"

"No, Mr. Spinner, I am not. When I tell you who the monkey was fused with, and what else is missing, you'll understand. But now I need that goddamn address. Please."

"Don't let him push you around," Charlie said. "Tell him that I don't want to give up the address."

"Charlie is not cooperating, Mr. Laos," I agreed with Charlie. "He is still mad at me, because I was rude to him."

"He might want money, Mr. Spinner. He's acting on your behalf. Good old greed. And here you have a rich man who is throwing money left and right, and you guys just can't miss an opportunity to secure ride on a gravy train. At this point I don't want to involve the authorities in this. Not yet. Let's try to resolve this privately. Ask Charlie how much?"

"Now he's talking," said Charlie. "Tell him a million would do."

"No, Charlie, I can't," I said embarrassed with my own greed.

"He wants a million, doesn't he?" Mr. Laos guessed, and I nodded. "Well, he'll get a million if we are successful," he said, and added, "and if we survive."

"Come on, it can't be that bad, can it?" I asked.

"We'll see. Could I have this damn address now, please?"

"Charlie?" I said. Thankfully Charlie spilled out the name and address without further delay. To anyone else it would look quite ordinary: Max Horn, P O Box 788711, Wheeling, IL 60090. But to me, it was anything but. Although the name Max Horn meant nothing to me, it left me surprised to say the least, because the Village of Wheeling was where my mother and grandmother lived. And Mr. Laos – he also looked astonished, and only said: "Shit! I should've known that!"

9

LYDIA and LUTZ

"Fasten your seat belt," Lydia reminded me, looking through the airplane window. "We are minutes away from landing."

I complied. I'd met Lydia only few hours earlier while boarding a rented mid-size jet, a Hawker 900, to bring us to Chicago's O'Hare airport. She joined Mr. Laos, Cho-Hu, Walter and me in a plane the rich man had booked using his cell phone.

When we arrived at a small private airport to take off for Chicago, Lydia was already waiting for us. She was introduced to me as Mr. Laos' assistant and confidant who worked on some scientific projects on the Island. She looked nice and friendly.

Nobody should think that I was forced to accompany this unusual team; I joined them on my own accord. Upon learning the details of what was at stake I practically begged Mr. Laos to allow me to be a part of the rescue team. My mother and grandmother were in the area, and I couldn't turn a blind eye to this fact. Depending on how badly things could develop, the population of the entire area could be in jeopardy, my relatives included.

What got me to where I was, happened shortly after I reacted to Mr. Laos's claim that he knew who Max Horn was.

"Well, who the hell is Max Horn?" I asked, eager to get more information.

Although I was familiar with the unpredictability of Mr. Laos' statements, his answer surprised me again.

"I don't really know," he said.

Typically surprising. I held my breath, expecting an explanation would follow. It did.

"We had an employee at Duke of Prunes, by the name Lutz Horn," Mr. Laos continued. "He was talented, a genius really, but quite secretive and eccentric. He once mentioned that he had a brother. I think this Max Horn could be that brother. Horn is not a common last name here, and for that particular cage to have a label with a person by that name hardly seems coincidental."

"Do you know anything more about him?"

"Who, Max? I never met the man, haven't seen his picture and I never heard anything more about him. But that's the only lead we have and let's hope he is Lutz's brother," Mr. Laos continued. He proceeded revealing some interesting but disturbing facts about Lutz.

I noticed that Mr. Laos referred to Lutz in the past tense, and I assumed it was because Lutz was no longer employed at Duke of Prunes. Maybe canned, maybe left on his own. One way or another, Lutz worked on the highly controversial biological warfare systems. They were military-controlled, top secret projects. Ventures were so problematic that the military pretended to know nothing about it. Lutz was formally employed by Mr. Laos' private enterprise, to shield the military from scandal if something went wrong and should Lutz's work somehow become known to the public. Lutz was involved with some projects which were banned by the Geneva Protocol international treaty and Biological Weapons Convention.

Lutz was a brilliant scientist and held two doctorates; in organic chemistry and evolutionary biology. He studied insect societies, particularly ants, and specifically how they communicate. Most information exchanged between the members of ant colonies are channeled through chemical substances called pheromones. Lutz discovered varieties and was developing more strains of pheromones. He managed to use them to switch insects into different modes, especially emphasizing aggression and territoriality. He successfully had them perform various tasks, including attacking live targets. Lutz learned to control the entire colony, making it perform potentially deadly assignments at his will. Using different mixtures of pheromones, he could pass signals to the entire colony and force it to behave in a desired manner.

Mr. Laos described to me an event where he witnessed a disturbing demonstration given by Lutz. The scientist made the ants viciously attack and kill a restrained mouse. The unexpected part was that Lutz was able to instruct the colony to direct their aggression on a selected target. Two mice were kept next to each other and Lutz asked Mr. Laos to choose which one should be spared. The grisly result was completed when the designated victim was entirely dismembered and eaten alive, while the other mouse came out of it intact and was totally ignored by the ant colony members, despite being kept in close proximity.

Lutz was described as an eccentric and overly emotional individual. He was not a team player and insisted working on his research alone. He had a bad temper and Mr. Laos saw him on occasion flying off the handle for minor problems and interruptions. He was demanding and didn't like restrictions in his requests for equipment, chemical materials, or supplies of ants and other living things.

For the longest time nobody knew that Lutz had a love affair with one female employee on the Island. An investigation later revealed it was a stormy relationship – mainly because of Lutz's working habits. He would work himself to exhaustion, and then would spend a few days recovering, requesting his girlfriend's presence and companionship during that time. She was not always able to comply, which would make Lutz angry. They would argue loudly, and Mr. Laos received reports of such incidents. This was how their relationship became common knowledge. During one such event, Lutz allegedly became enraged and investigation showed that, to demonstrate to the lady in question just how much he was upset, he committed suicide.

According to Mr. Laos it was never clear whether Lutz intended to go ahead with his suicide attempt, or he killed himself accidentally. He left a detailed letter of instructions specifying what to do in case of his death. It stated that if his brain remained biologically usable, he wanted it to be fused with a lab monkey, to create another fanimal. He singled out a mandrill from the lab as the one he wanted to be fused with. That animal was a specimen of a very social species and was used on research in how depravation of social life affects their behavior. This particular individual was adapting very well to being deprived of social contacts.

After much discussion it was decided to honor Lutz's wish because his research and results were of importance. He had left no information about his results, neither on paper, nor in his computer. There was no way to pick up from where he had left off and continue the work he pioneered. So, Lutz was successfully fused with the mandrill and pressed into creating a record of his discoveries. Lydia was one of the scientists who was involved in this project.

All this occurred shortly prior to closing down the Duke of Prunes facility. Shipping cages were all labeled with a Kansas address. Apparently, nobody noticed that the cage in which the fanimal Lutz/mandrill was housed had a different address on its label. This cage never made it to Kansas, and, thanks to Charlie's information, Mr. Laos was convinced that it wound up in Illinois – delivered to Max Horn, Lutz' brother.

Mr. Laos said another container was also missing, one very much connected to Lutz and his research.

"Let me guess," I interrupted. "The missing container held a bunch of ants, and you are worried he might release them on the Chicagoland human population."

As fascinating as what I'd learn sounded to me, I was somewhat skeptical about the level of danger this presented to a large number of humans. Why such a big fuss – if these crazed ants attack humans, all that needed to be done was to burn them down before they could spread and do further damage. In my estimate, the overall harm they could do to us was limited.

"I wish it was that simple, Mr. Spinner," Mr. Laos said. "But I'm afraid it's not so. The missing container holds no ants but living colonies of different germs. You see, Lutz began his experiments with ant colonies, but later extended his research to microbes and viruses. We are talking about not only the deadliest kind but also newly created strains of bacteria. The pheromone is a substance that microcolonies of microbes and viruses also use for some sort of communication. If Lutz established control over them the same way he demonstrated what he could do with ants, and chooses to exercise similar tasks with them, God help us. He is a very unpredictable man. I don't know what he is going to do, but in these crazy times we live in, I can't rule anything out. I know that he has created some new strain of anthrax, and the Lassa virus. Nasty little buggers. We have no way to fight them off, and I hate to think what could happen if they are unleashed and encouraged to turn on us. If that happens, they might be unstoppable."

10

MAX and NIGHT

It was the middle of the night when we approached Max Horn's house. I have never before burglarized nor broke into anyone's home and this was quite distressing for me.

Charlie was a nervous wreck. "Spinner, I don't like it. I just don't like it."

I didn't like it either. But Walter and Cho-Hu didn't seem to have a problem with what we were doing.

"Any dogs in the house?" Walter quietly asked.

"No," Alex answered. "One man, I suppose Max, and an aquarium with a few fish."

Wait, wait! Alex? Fanimal Alex, a dog with a human brain?

Yes, that's right.

What the hell was Alex doing in Wheeling, Illinois, and how did he get there? I know, I shouldn't run ahead of myself, so I better take it from where I left off.

Some hours earlier we landed at Chicago's O'Hare airport and I watched the plane slowing down and rolling over the tarmac toward an obscure unmarked terminal, reserved for passengers of private airplanes, away from the crowded main terminals.

As we approached, Charlie became nervous. "Spinner don't get involved. You can't help much anyway. Excuse yourself and leave. You can tell them that you're sick."

But I can't leave, Charlie. With all these people around, I couldn't talk back to Charlie. Lydia was glued to me. I bet Mr. Laos asked her to keep her eye on me.

"I know what you're thinking," Charlie continued. "You don't want to be viewed as a sissy. Think about it. You can't help much, and if disaster happens you will be up shit creek. It's time to think about saving your own ass."

I wanted to answer that I knew all that, but I just couldn't chicken out. I also had to think about my mother and grandmother. Yes, I was scared. I always tried to minimize risks. This time everything was completely out of my control. My mind's warning bells and lights were ringing and flashing, my brain was switched to Defcon 2 mode, but there was nothing I could do to control the situation. Besides, Cho-Hu and Walter were in the same predicament, and they didn't seem to mind or complain. Even Mr. Laos didn't run away. I couldn't stop thinking what if that damn container holding the viruses was opened and viruses began infecting everything around them? And we were getting closer and closer to it. Mr. Laos said, both, the container must be located, as well as Lutz, the crazy fanimal monkey. Mr. Laos pointed out that if Lutz wouldn't cooperate, he would have to be terminated before he could turn the germs on us. Mr. Laos used poetic terminology – which I found inappropriate for the situation, by stating 'the threat must be eliminated before the wrath of the mandrill was unleashed.'

Mr. Laos was determined to find Lutz and the container. He was obviously trying to save his own ass, because alerting the authorities about this would put on the line everything he had. Letting the dubious experimental crazy fanimal escape, having this damn container with contagious microorganisms missing, endangering the public, failing to share information with the authorities in a timely fashion – all those were the crimes he might be accused of committing.

"Why don't we let the FBI, military or whomever, handle this?" I'd asked him earlier.

"I am responsible for what happened, and I should fix it myself. If we fail, I will alert the military, you can bet I will."

Mister, if we fail, it will be too late to go to the military, I thought, but said nothing. By that time, they would already be well aware of the crisis.

The airplane came to a full stop, and we stepped out. We approached a small building that was the private terminal for VIPs, and in front of it I saw standing... oh my God – Petra! And next to her, a large dog, an Irish Wolfhound, Alex. How the hell? Was I hallucinating?

"I brought them here," Mr. Laos rushed to explain. "He might be of help, and Miss Petra agreed to pretend owning the dog."

Petra opened her arms and hugged me. I sensed she was not too thrilled with me.

"Hello, Spinner," she said sounding colder than usual.

I didn't respond. It looked like she'd had it with me. She must have been angry for what I'd done. My stupid plot to kidnap Elizabeth! How foolish! However, the newest situation had nothing to do with me. I hadn't cooked it up. She should know that, and at least give me credit for being there and trying to help. Hey, I was a good guy for once.

I was wondering, were there more surprises coming up? What's next – perhaps Mrs. Miller in her wheelchair waiting for us in the building, with a rifle in her lap? Luckily, not.

We entered a small foyer. Everyone had to use the bathroom.

Then Mr. Laos said, "I checked on Lutz's brother, Max. I have the address of his house in Wheeling, and we are going to pay him a visit. The container might be there. As far as Lutz, I have a good idea of his whereabouts. Max works at the Chicago Zoo, as a curator of primates. This is why Lutz wanted to be fused with a monkey. I bet Lutz is in the zoo. Looking like a mandrill he blends with the zoo's existing monkey residents. But first, we must get Max to tell us where the container is."

And so, Walter, Cho-Hu, myself and Alex hopped into the large rented van, while Petra, Mr. Laos and Lydia went to the hotel where they were supposed to wait for our return. Cho-Hu drove following the GPS instructions, and took us straight to the address where Max was living. The street was well lit, revealing a quiet residential neighborhood with nice houses and mature trees covering both sides of the avenue. The house had a front yard fenced off with a four-foot-tall decorative fence. The gate was latched from the inside and opened with no problem. We followed the paved narrow trail to the front porch and the front door.

Breaking into the house was a piece of cake, when you had an expert like Walter at hand. When Alex assured us there were no dogs in the house, Walter skillfully unlocked the door. He was a true pro.

With Alex's guidance and Walter's flashlight, we carefully entered the home's hallway and found our way to the bedroom. We quietly surrounded the bed where a person was sleeping. Cho-Hu woke him up by covering the man's mouth with his hand and pinning him down in the bed with his body, while Walter switched on the room light.

As expected, Max, suddenly awakened in such manner, reacted in panic, tried to scream and jump up from the bed, but Cho-Hu wouldn't let go. Max gave up and stopped fighting sooner than I would have predicted.

"Max, we're here to talk," Walter quickly said. "Don't panic, we won't harm you."

The man relaxed, and Cho-Hu released his grip on him. Max sat in the bed and looked at us, nodding.

"I guess I expected something like this might happen," he said. "You are here because of my brother, right?"

Walter, who took the role of main interrogator, quickly said, "we know that you are keeping him in the zoo, together with other monkeys. We want the container that was shipped at the same time your brother came to you."

Max focused on Alex.

"Are you a fanimal too?" he asked. "I see your skull is also deformed. Can you talk?"

Alex looked at me, and I nodded.

"Yes," Alex confirmed.

"This is incredible. What you people do on Duke of Prunes is fascinating," Max said. "My brother foolishly killed himself but is practically resurrected in the form of a mandrill. I'm keeping him separately from the others, because he's freaking them out. They'd like to kill him. He is freaking me out too – he was always a black sheep in the family. The weirdest, the smartest, the craziest."

"Do you know what is in the container he sent you?" Walter asked.

"Not really, he only told me that inside was the result of his discoveries and experiments."

"What's in it is dangerous and could potentially spread and kill many. We need to know where it is, and what your brother intends to do with it," Walter said, sounding impatient.

"When he arrived, the first thing he wanted was that container," Max said.

"And?"

"I gave it to him. It belongs to him; I had no idea. He keeps it in his cage."

"We have to get it," Walter said.

"He's a very angry man, or should I say monkey. We should talk to him. We can all go there."

Walter retreated to a corner of the room and made a call on his cell phone. He spoke shortly and quietly. When his conversation was over, he turned back to us: "He will meet us at the zoo. If we take off right away, we can arrive before the zoo opens. Let's go."

"He, who?" Max wanted to know.

"It doesn't make any difference, you don't know him," Walter said. "Get ready."

Max jumped from the bed to put his clothes on, while we went to a living room, leaving only Alex to watch that Max didn't do anything stupid.

The man seemed to be cooperating, and shortly thereafter we took off for the zoo in our rented van.

The first rays of sunrise colored the clouds in the sky reddish like blood, as if announcing what the upcoming day might bring.

11

MATHILDA and REVENGE

We loaded ourselves into the van, and Max gave the address to Cho-Hu, our driver, who entered the data into the GPS: "It's a 40-minute ride, guys." He started the engine and merged into the light early morning traffic.

Walter took a seat next to Cho-Hu, and Max sat in the second row with me, while Alex comfortably rode in the back.

Walter got on the phone with Mr. Laos, while I took the opportunity to learn more about Max's brother. Before I could say anything, Charlie interrupted: "You might want to get some information about his brother."

As usual, almost every time Charlie opened his imaginary mouth, he got on my nerves. He treated me like I was a child needing his advice for just about everything. He must think I'm dumb as a doorknob. This was irritating, and I had to suppress my anger.

"Tell me more about Lutz," I said to Max, ignoring Charlie.

Max paused and took a deep breath before answering. "Youknow, we were never very close. When we split after growing up together, we communicated only sporadically. I know he is a bright scientist who worked on secret zoological projects on an island off the Atlantic coast. Lately he initiated more frequent contacts with me. He kept complaining about Mathilda and wanted to know everything about my work with primates."

"Who is Mathilda?"

"His girlfriend. It surprised me that he even had one. As a child he constantly feuded with our mother. He hated her. I thought he would never have a relationship with any woman."

"Why did he hate his mother?"

"She was a difficult person and treated both of us harshly, but especially him. She kept picking on Lutz, especially after having her daily strawberry vodka lemonade cocktail. He was born out of a stormy relationship our mother had with a violent man. He is now in jail for murder. I think Lutz was conceived in a rape situation, and mother was never able to get over it and accept him. I have a different father, so Lutz is my half-brother. We were never close. I remember him being withdrawn, arrogant and hostile as a child."

"This Lutz person is a psycho," Charlie rushed to warn me. "You better watch out for this one."

Yes Charlie, thank you for your insight. I could never have figure that out without you. Otherwise I might think that Lutz could turn into a regular Mr. Rogers, if he had only been raised in the right neighborhood – I was thinking sarcastically.

"What did your brother want to know about your work?" I asked.

"He became excited when I told him that we also have mandrills in our primate collection. He said that if something bad happened to him, he might have his brain experimentally merged with a mandrill they had on the Island, and that animal would be sent to me. I was shocked. He sounded fanatical and suicidal. Knowing him I figured there was a good chance this could really happen. But when I received the crate with a mandrill I freaked out when he began speaking to me. His brain is really a part of the mandrill's body. I convinced my staff that the animal was brought in from another zoo for possible breeding. He had a hard time refraining from talking in front of other people. Other mandrills in the troop didn't accept him, and nobody questioned why he had to be kept separated."

"What does he really want?"

"Not sure – all I know is that he is very angry. The container you guys are asking me about is hidden amongst the straw bales in his cage. You sure something bad could happen?"

"He worked on some obscure germ projects and he might have produced new strains of a very contagious bacteria," I tried to explain.

"And there is no cure yet, right?" I nodded, and Max paused. "I agree – he should be stopped," he finally said.

"Yes, if he releases the little buggers from the container it could wreak havoc."

"And he might. He is emotionally unstable and upset. He gets easily excited. I think he regrets he is no longer human. I have to calm him down every time I talk to him. Adrenaline overdrive. I think his breakup with Mathilda pushed him over the edge. You guys have your work cut out for you."

This sounded bad. Here we had an angry deranged person trapped in a monkey's body, a paranoid individual who controlled germs that could do harm if let loose. He was crazy, and I was even crazier – heading straight toward the threat. Not smart. Not smart at all. I expected Charlie to butt in with his two cents, but he remained surprisingly quiet.

Walter turned toward us. "Lydia will be waiting for us at the zoo entrance."

"What about Petra?" Alex asked.

"I don't think she'll be joining us, nor Mr. Laos. Billionaires seldom do things – they direct others to do them. He will be close by, though."

Cho-Hu drove and turned the van into a side street, parking close to an inconspicuous door reserved for zoo personnel. It blended with the same color paint on the wall and was partially covered with climbing plants.

We stepped out from the van and met Lydia who was already waiting there. She looked miserable, dressed too light for the chilly Chicago morning, and carrying an oversized purse.

"Thank God, you're finally here," she started. "I'm freezing my ass off! They dropped me here 20 minutes early. People are looking at me suspiciously."

"Sorry about that," Cho-Hu said.

"It's not your fault, I'm just venting," Lydia said impatiently. "Shall we go in now?"

"Sure," Walter said. "Cho-Hu and Alex, you guys stay here and wait for us."

Max unlocked the employee entrance and we entered the zoo grounds. He took us deeper inside the zoo, to an old building with a sign 'Primate House' on it. We entered the building through a side door and found ourselves inside a much larger interior than it looked from outside.

Cages on the left and right. It was warm and smelly, and reminded me of what I'd seen at Duke of Prunes. Max went toward the end of the hall. As we passed by the cages, the monkeys housed in them saw us and started vocalizing, louder and louder, banging on the metal and screaming from the top of their lungs at us. Their racket became incredibly loud, almost unbearable. This was creepy and made me uncomfortable. If Petra was here, she would be petrified.

"Pay no attention to them!" Max shouted. "They are always this noisy."

This was easier said than done. Walter also nervously looked around, as though expecting a monkey attack. Lydia sped up, passing the cages as fast as possible. Max unlocked one door. Inside was a room roughly divided in half, with heavy, double fencing installed from floor to ceiling and wall to wall. Inside the cage, in one corner, I saw a fanimal, mandrill/Lutz. He was looking back at us.

I observed the creature. The mandrill had a striking face, with a red stripe down his nose, framed with blue flanges. This fanimal also had a grotesque extension on the back of his head, added to house Lutz's brain, making it similar in appearance to Alex's head.

His eyes looked penetratingly sharp and intelligent. I couldn't say if this was how mandrills' eyes really were, or whether the look was enhanced with the addition of a human brain.

"It's OK, Lutz," Max rushed to calm down his brother, who stood up taking a hostile posture. "It's OK to talk."

"No, it's not OK," he said in a rusty voice, resembling Alex's. "What do you want?"

"It's me, Lydia."

"I remember who you are, I'm not stupid. My memory is still with me. Stop staring at me," Lutz said belligerently.

"Why?"

"Without clothes I feel naked," he said, "I don't like women watching me."

"But you are naked, Lutz," Lydia said, suppressing a smile.

Lutz returned to his corner, sat, and angrily repeated: "What do you want?"

"Information. What will you do with the container, and why did you escape from Duke of Prunes?" Lydia continued.

"I'm sick of you, that's why. I don't want to go to Kansas. Whoever decided to shut down Duke of Prunes is an idiot. Nothing was broken, and they went to fix it anyway. And, Mathilda wouldn't go, either. She decided to go back to Oklahoma, because her sister was sick. Irritating. I completed my research – I'm ready for testing."

"Testing, what?"

"I'm dead already, anyway. You think that living in a cage, in a mandrill's body and naked satisfies me? I want to see my revenge at work. Then I can die for good."

Revenge? This struck a resonant note. I was obsessed by revenge myself, and it ended almost catastrophically for me. This was not good. This guy was crazy and ready for anything. Blinded by revenge, he was in a position to do more damage than I ever could. Yes, he should be stopped.

"Revenge is not the way to go, believe me. Forgiveness is," I tried.

"Who the hell are you? A preacher? You don't look like a preacher, you look like a schmuck," the fanimal fired back.

He was right about that. I felt like a schmuck, but his comment angered me.

"Who are you seeking revenge against?" Walter asked.

"Don't try to analyze me, you moron! Go back to your boss and stick to your gorilla job," Lutz continued with insults, showing his huge canine teeth.

I knew we needed to calm Lutz down, and get him to surrender that bloody container, but so far everything that was said only seemed to aggravate him more.

"C'mon, you're not stupid," I said, trying to sound calm and reasonable. "You can't hold grudges against everything and everyone. You know that this type of generalizing is wrong."

"There goes the damn preacher turning psychiatrist. Or, political correctness activist. What do you know about generalizing? You don't even know what you're talking about," he said in a hostile voice.

"It's your mother, right?" Walter asked.

"It's women in general, right?" Lydia jumped in.

Well, this didn't go well, but only added to Lutz's outrage. The guy went mad.

"Shut up, you assholes! What do you know about my mother? Damn it, Max, why did you bring these idiots to me? What did you tell them about me?"

"Easy, Lutz, don't go nuts now," Max answered, and turned to us, "not good, not good, don't challenge him and don't keep upsetting him. Please."

"And don't look him in the eyes, or at his tiny privates either," Lydia returned the insult.

Lutz went berserk. He charged the fence and hit it hard, making us jump back toward the door. The fencing was strong enough to remain in place even after such a violent attack. My heart was pounding, and I wondered what in the world Lydia was trying to do.

"Shut your mouth, you fucking ovulating cunt! You'll be the first one to find out if I generalize or not. You bitch – you will be the first to pay. It's only double 'x' I target, nothing else."

What the hell was a double 'x'? I had no idea, but Lydia seemed to know. Her explanation came as Lutz jumped back toward the middle of his cage, where he pulled out from the straw a small container and opened it.

"Chromosomes, he's talking about chromosomes. Double 'x' defines the female gender," Lydia quickly explained.

"Yes, and you, bitch, are one of them," an enraged Lutz shouted and pulled from the container a small wooden case with vials. He then forcefully threw the case toward us and it hit the fence, breaking in pieces. Some vials shattered and whatever was in them became airborne. Max screamed 'no!' but before we could do anything else, Lydia quickly pulled from her oversized purse a bottle. I instantly recognized it was a Molotov cocktail. I saw in horror how she used a cigarette lighter to ignite the cloth wick sticking from the top of the bottle's neck. The next moment she threw the bottle on the fence. It broke with a loud crackling noise and a vapor cloud of released fuel in the bottle exploded, causing a fireball, flying everywhere, spreading flaming droplets to both sides of the fence. Some landed on the straw and some on Lutz. He screamed in dismay, and jumped back, trying to avoid the flaming projectiles. The loose hay in his cage where the droplets landed immediately began smoldering and some turned into small flames. The smell of kerosene filled the space.

This happened in an instant and all I could do was to scream and instinctively try to flee the room. Yes, I panicked. The others did too. Who wouldn't? We all rushed out, shutting the door behind us.

In the hall I became aware of noises coming from the monkeys caged there. They must have sensed something bad was going on and their screaming and banging against metal doors and other objects was incredible, causing pandemonium in my head. A fire alarm went off adding to the chaotic situation.

"What did you do, Lydia?" I shouted.

"I had to," she shouted back.

I saw a fire extinguisher enclosed in a glass case on the wall. I broke it with my elbow and grabbed the extinguisher, taking it back toward the door behind which Lutz was caged.

"Spinner, don't," Charlie said in his pathetic voice, but I was acting on impulse.

"I'm going back."

"For Pete's sake, he is my brother, I'm with you," Max said and went after me.

Walter seemed to be undecided, but Lydia backed away, shaking her head. "I can't. The son of a bitch may have infected me already, I won't risk more. You should be OK – he targets only females."

"Don't do it, Spinner," Charlie repeated.

"Shut up!" I yelled, reaching the door. I kicked it with my foot as hard as I could, and the damn thing flew wide open.

12

CAROL and HELEN

In a fraction of a second, while the door was opening, through my mind momentarily flashed the hope that I would see standing there Mr. Laos, Petra, Walter, Cho-Hu and Lydia – all of them smiling and yelling in unison 'surprise!' – and I would learn that everything was only another clever prank pulled again on me. This would indeed be my preferred option over a bleak reality promising nothing but misery, harm and death.

Wishful thinking! As the door opened wide, heavy smoke burst through the doorway dispersing any doubts about what was really going on. A thick pungent scent invaded my eyes and nostrils, and I started tearing up and coughing. I could hardly see or breathe. Even though I had a strong urge to turn around and get the hell out of there, I proceeded stepping into the room. There were two fire sprinklers on the ceiling puking pathetic amounts of water – not enough to put the fire out but at least slow down its spreading. Lutz's cage was immersed in flames and smoke, and through them I saw the monkey, face down on the floor in the furthest corner of his enclosure, motionless, as though dead. I somehow managed to get the fire extinguisher working and began spraying the flames through the fence into the cage. The extinguisher functioned well, suffocating the flames wherever the foam touched them, but producing additional smoke and irritating my throat and eyes even more.

Max passed me in an attempt to unlock the cage. Charlie produced more advice in his emotionless, irritating voice. "You better get the hell out of here."

The building's fire alarm was earsplitting, and, mixed with the sound of emergency vehicles and their sirens in the distance, as well as screams of petrified monkeys in other cages, created a chaotic audio scene. I started gasping for air and turned around, realizing I couldn't take more of the smoke, when I tripped over something on the floor. I fell down and blacked out.

§

I don't know how long I was unconscious, but when I opened my eyes, I found myself laying down flat, stretched in a narrow, comfortable bed, later identified as a hyperbaric oxygen chamber. The entire bed was surrounded by one gigantic clear plastic tube and equipped with several peculiar attachments whose purposes I couldn't figure out. The bed was in the middle of a small, portable isolation room with walls made of some kind of flexible semitransparent material. I felt slightly claustrophobic. I would soon learn that the entire zoo's Primate House and its immediate surroundings were closed off, converted into a quarantine zone, set up by first responders after the fire started. Apparently, somebody informed the authorities about the possibility that the airborne pathogens of an unknown origin might be contaminating the area. This was the place where I was treated for inhaling carbon monoxide. My poisoning was luckily less severe than I feared. I was to be kept in isolation until it was determined if I was contaminated with who knew what kind of germs released by Lutz. The tube around my bed was closed off on one side, but, the other side, where my feet were, was actually a circular door, and it was open.

The isolation unit must have been under observation, because as soon as I began moving toward the open end of the tube, and attempted to get out, a person appeared, wearing, what seemed like an astronaut's spacesuit. They told me later it was a level A protective biohazard outfit. To me this was an obvious sign that I was infected with Lutz's damn viruses, and that I was soon going to die. I was upset, panicky, feeling weak and sick.

"How much time do I have?" I asked the astronaut.

"We don't know," the female voice answered. "We don't know yet if you are even contaminated."

I took a better look at this person. Her gear included steel shanked boots, protective gloves, a two-way radio and a breathing apparatus incorporated inside her suit. When she spoke, her voice came out of a speaker mounted in one corner of the room.

Her name was lieutenant Carol Mallory-Gonzaga, and other than that she never explained her own position and role in any of this. My communication with her was predominantly a one-way street. This was disappointing. They wanted to know everything about me, and my association with the event. How did I get involved and what was my role? I realized that I should tell the truth. After all, I didn't do anything wrong. For once I was the good guy here. For crying out loud, I tried to put out the fire and save the fanimal. I almost died in this attempt. Perhaps this would qualify me as a hero – at least in my own eyes?

Charlie gave me good advice regarding what to tell them. I said the Duke of Prunes Island was a location where a motion picture was shot. I was part of that movie. I didn't admit that initially I wasn't aware I was an actor in the film – this would be embarrassing and, I figured, entirely irrelevant anyway. Somebody on the Island discovered that one fanimal – Lutz, a disgruntled scientist fused with a mandrill – escaped. They found out that Max, Lutz's brother, hid Lutz in the zoo. Mr. Laos, who was a big shot on the Island, asked me if I'd like to join the team assembled to go after Lutz because they feared he might let loose germs he had created. I didn't know why Mr. Laos asked me to join them, but I agreed, because my mother was a resident of the area where the zoo was located. After Lutz threw something at us, Lydia started a fire, and I grabbed the fire extinguisher to put it out but was overwhelmed with smoke and passed out. I expected no medal, but a simple 'thank you' would be nice. There.

"Who is Lydia?" Carol asked.

Charlie immediately alerted me. "Careful here. Maybe they do have Lydia and want to confirm your association with her. But if she escaped, perhaps they don't even know who she is."

Right. I didn't know what else to say, or who I should protect, and how. I didn't know what was going on, only what I'd done.

"I don't know. I told you all I know. I don't want to repeat myself. I don't know anything else. If I am not infected and contagious, I'd like to just get the hell out of here."

Carol didn't further insist and suggested that I rest and be patient.

During the next few days they did lots of testing on me. Some things were rather uncomfortable and embarrassing. The bubble where I was kept captive featured a total lack of privacy. More than anything, it bothered me that my questions weren't answered, and nobody visited me. I felt abandoned and kept in the dark. They wouldn't even let me know if there was an outbreak of deadly pathogens out there and people were dropping like flies. Or was the hysteria over the event much exaggerated and everything was really fine. Or something in between.

On my third day there, Petra visited. She talked to me from the other side of my room wall, speaking into a microphone. She must have been told not to update me about the current situation, because she was rather short with me and appeared somewhat distant. She said they told her I would be let go the next day because all indicators showed that I wasn't infected. This was good news. I said that I would like to visit my mother and I would like Petra to join me. She agreed and left.

Carol came in before I was let go and finally provided a little information. Lutz unfortunately died from smoke inhalation. Several female monkeys in the Primate House also died. Some got sick and recovered on their own, and some showed no signs of illness at all. It seemed that the virus targeted only females. The virus was isolated and found to be only moderately risky. Luckily it wasn't spread around very easily. Lutz's creation was not entirely as he expected. The virus would attach itself to the infected person's uterus, causing illness and resulting in infertility. This made me think of Lydia. Was she in their custody, or had she somehow escaped and was walking freely around? She was patient zero, the first person who could have caught the disease, and if she was running around and spreading it, I should maybe tell them about her.

Charlie suggested that I not tell. "It's a can of worms. Don't open it. If you do, they'll keep you here longer, and ask more questions. They will also want to know why you didn't tell them about it earlier. They might find you responsible if Lydia is spreading the sickness around."

I agreed. After all, they were short with me too. I'd given them what they asked. No more, no less. I didn't know why they never asked more questions about Lydia, but luckily, they didn't. Most likely, this wasn't an issue.

§

I was finally let go, escorted from the quarantine area and through the zoo exit. Outside, a taxi waited for me, and in it Petra. Thank God, everything looked normal. I saw people walking their dogs, mothers pushing strollers, and children playing. There was a sign on the zoo wall stating, 'Closed for renovations – sorry for the inconvenience.'

I sat next to Petra in the back seat and gave the driver my mother's address. I borrowed Petra's cell phone and called my mother, to let her know we were coming for a visit. Mom was characteristically unimpressed with my call and complained that I should have called more in advance so she could pick up the house a bit, especially if I was bringing a guest.

"So, what's going on?" I asked Petra. "I was kept in the dark for days. Where is Lydia?"

Petra pointed with her eyes toward the taxi driver, letting me know that she wouldn't openly answer my questions. I got it. Whatever happened would not be made known to the public, and obviously the consequences of the event were minute. Our driver acted as if he didn't know much about anything extraordinary happening and Petra wanted it to stay that way. I had no problem with that.

Petra answered, in general terms, that Lydia was fine, and recovering. They were monitoring her condition, and it looked like she was going to be okay.

"Who are 'they'?" I asked.

"You know, Mr. Laos and his medical team," she answered.

I also asked where Alex was.

"He's back in Kansas," Petra surprised me.

"I thought you had custody over him," I said.

"I'll explain later," she said and again pointed toward the taxi driver. "I'm a bit tired, you know."

I understood. We spent the rest of our ride not talking. I only asked Petra if she was mad at me. She said we should talk when we were at my mother's house. She must have been infuriated when she found out that my announced visit to my mother was a lie, and instead I went to Duke of Prunes to carry out my crazy childish kidnapping adventure. And now, as one of life's ironic coincidences, we both were on our way to visit my mother anyway, albeit under different circumstances.

Our taxi pulled over and parked in front of my mother's modest house. My mother must have been on the lookout because she immediately opened the door and stepped out. Her hair was grey, she looked older, skinnier and shorter than I remembered her.

"Good to see you, Spinner," she stated, and gave me a hug.

"You too, Mom," I said and pointed to Petra: "This is my girlfriend, Petra."

"Nice to meet you," Petra said and extended her hand. Mother nodded and after a handshake invited us into the house.

"Please sit, make yourself comfortable," she offered, entering the small living room, furnished with outdated and unmatched furniture. The room was cluttered with predominantly religious knickknacks. "How long has it been?"

"Don't remind me," I said. "I know – I've been a bad boy. Seldom calling, seldom visiting."

"At least you know that we are doing fairly well, praise the Lord. Otherwise you would have heard from me, all right? Speaking of being well, why don't you say hello to your grandma? She is fading away."

And mother pointed to a hall leading toward other rooms.

My grandmother, Helen, was laying in her bed, covered from head to toe, with only her sleeping wrinkled face visible. Mother pulled grandma's hand from under the bedding and invited me to hold her hand.

"She can feel you're here, Spinner," mother said. Grandma's hand was bony and cold. Touching her wasn't as uncomfortable as I had expected, and I said a few words to her, and it looked like she heard me because she smiled a bit, but never opened her eyes.

Back in the living room we continued our conversation which shortly turned awkward. Typical for my mother. Without much hesitation she asked how much longer we planned to live in sin before we tied the knot, as sanctification was the will of God. I refrained from reminding her that she had me out of wedlock, and that her preaching was not totally appropriate. But this would only open old wounds. This kind of discussion made both Petra and I uncomfortable. I didn't want to get into an argument with Mom, so I asked if she would make us a cup of tea.

She went to the kitchen and I turned to Petra.

"Now you know why I don't contact her often."

"Sure," Petra said. "Spinner, I need to tell you something."

By the tone of her voice I realized this was not going to be pleasant. I said: "Go ahead."

"You remember asking me about Alex, and was surprised when I told you that he was in Kansas?"

I nodded.

"Well, Mr. Laos offered me a job there, to continue custody over Alex, and become the head of security. He also agreed that I be a liaison between the facility and 3ACS and oversee the treatment of the animals there. My views are not so radical as 3ACS' but they accepted my making sure the animals there are treated as humanly as possible."

What? She didn't have to tell me that she accepted the offer – it was obvious. But, what about me? She didn't even ask if I would be willing to relocate.

"What about me?" I questioned.

Petra hesitated for a moment and looked aside. "Spinner, you know that our relationship could never be described as a passionate love story. Yes, we love each other, and we've been through a lot together. The thing is I just couldn't adjust to having both you and Charlie in my life."

What? She knew that I communicated with Charlie, even though I did my best to hide this from her? At this point I really didn't know what to say or how to react. While my mother was talking marriage, I was being dumped. Then came the last nail in the coffin of my relationship with Petra.

"There is something else, Spinner. Please don't be mad. It looks like Mr. Laos and I are going to be an item."

What? Jealousy caused blood rushed into my head, and I felt like I was going to explode, while my entire world was crumbling. He was older than her, almost old enough to be her father. And he was a billionaire. It figured.

"Did you sleep with him?" was my next question, even though I knew whatever the answer was, it was irrelevant – and it wouldn't change anything. And yet, I hoped that she had enough decency and respect for me, not to have sex with that man – at least not before she properly dumped me. And now, when she did – she was free to go.

Before Petra could answer my question, my mother showed up with a tea tray and cookies. We drank in awkward silence. I didn't think my mother overheard our conversation, but our demeanor let her figure out that something dramatic must have happened between Petra and me, so luckily, she toned down her religious rhetoric.

There came a strange noise from grandmother's room, and Mom went to check on her.

Alone again, I asked again if she had slept with him.

"What difference does it make?" Petra said. "But, if you need to know, yes, I did. I am so sorry to hurt you."

I felt sick to my stomach. I must have loved Petra more than I realized. What I heard was painful.

"He told me to let you know he will make good on financial arrangements you two had with each other."

Whatever. I was a millionaire now, but it didn't make me feel any better. At that moment I became painfully aware that, how true, money can't buy you happiness. This only worsened when my mother came back from grandma's room and announced: "Grandma Helen is now in God's hands. She died peacefully and with a smile, which you put on her face, Spinner."

I was completely wiped out by all this, and I felt like crying. My mother said that she was prepared for the death of her 92-year-old mother and had everything under control. She didn't need any help from us. She was practically kicking us out.

Before we knew it, we found ourselves out on the street in the front of her house.

Petra phoned and called two taxis. She had already moved out from our apartment and left all my things there. She gave me the keys and a credit card to buy a ticket back home.

One taxi arrived first, and she jumped in it.

"Take care, Spinner," she said and disappeared.

I was waiting for my taxi, feeling numb and low.

"I never liked her much," Charlie said.

"Shut up, Charlie," I said.

"I know how you feel, man," he continued.

"No, you don't," I said.

"Yes, I do," he insisted. "We are one and the same, remember?"

"All right," I said. "Since you are so smart, what do I do now? Any advice?"

"Yes," he answered. "Stay vertical. That's all. Stay vertical, Spinner."

I saw in the distance a taxi approaching. A raindrop landed on my hand and I looked into the sky. It was cloudy and it was going to rain. My cab pulled in front of me, and the driver came out and opened the back door inviting me in. This was good. I beat the rain – I won't even get wet. I stayed vertical.

PART 2: DAMAGE CONTROL

13

CAT and ENVELOPE

Frequently checking the balance on my bank account made me feel a bit better, although not entirely. My primary source of pain was, of course, Petra breaking up with me. But the death of my grandmother was also causing me, somewhat surprisingly, to mourn and uncharacteristically reminisce about my life, past, family and lack of 'career.'

Here I was – in my mid-thirties, and the only family I had was my mother. Too bad, we were not very close, neither physically, nor emotionally. I also had a friend, Joe, but I was seeing him less and less. My collaboration with his mother was a strange one and left her son and me feeling somewhat coarse. It was he who described her as being a bit 'psycho' and when I confirmed this firsthand, he seemed to be uncomfortable with that. My cat was housed in Joe's garage, obviously belonging to him more than to me. This had also become an issue with me. I thought, here I was, unable even to take care of my cat. Then there was Charlie, my alter-ego, with whom I argued more than I had expected. I became aware that too much communicating with him could be dangerous to my mental health. I had to be careful and not let my alter-ego pushes me to become diagnosed with a multiple personality disorder. I wondered why I had to speak loudly in order for Charlie to hear me, and why couldn't he know what I was thinking. I worried if this was normal. Was I already going crazy? Luckily, at least I never tried to cure my periodic depression and feeling of emptiness by becoming an alcoholic or taking drugs or mind-altering chemicals. I never had the affinity to use them as means of escaping from reality. A cold glass of beer here and there was good enough for me.

I successfully resisted the urge to get more information about the new Kansas facility that had been moved from Duke of Prunes Island, where Petra relocated, worked and had a relationship with Mr. Laos. I canceled the apartment Petra and I shared because everything there reminded me of her. I couldn't stand being there on my own – and the place was way too big for me anyway. I was proud that I'd tried to save that fanimal Lutz/mandrill, practically risking my own life when I entered the flaming room and tried to put the fire out. But I also couldn't forget how I was tricked again when I attempted to retaliate by kidnapping the daughter of Mr. Laos. This mixture of feelings turned me away from thinking about the past very often. Charlie's suggestion to stay vertical was sound advice – not to let depression put me down.

I moved into a nice two-bedroom apartment in Ceilings. I selected it according to my old habits – privacy first, with thick walls, multiple building exits, and tenants who were predominantly working-class younger professionals and not too friendly, minding their own business. Naturally, before everything I checked the cleanliness of the place and verified the absence of spiders and bugs.

Money was no longer an object. Mr. Laos deposited funds directly into my bank account according to our deal, and I was now technically a millionaire. Keeping the majority in a single savings account with a minimal interest rate drove the bank manager crazy, and the only way I could stop the bank's attempts to hook me up with a financial advisor was to threaten to pull out all my money and go elsewhere, unless they left me alone and stopped contacting me with their offers. I stressed that the privacy was the most important issue for me. I told them that the money was the result of a business deal and the income would be properly reported and taxes were already paid – which was the truth. They finally left me alone. As a convenience I opened their credit card. I was using it often, to create a buffer between my money and those I was paying. I would pay off the entire credit card balance every month.

I did call my mother to hear if she received the funds I sent her to help with funeral and burial expenses for grandma Helen. I offered to send more but she thanked me and said I didn't have to send her anything – she had everything under control. She then inquired about Petra and stated that she liked her and would be happy to see us 'tying the knot' soon. She was very disappointed when I told her that we split shortly after our visit.

I spent some time trying to organize myself and figure out what I wanted to do. Charlie was mostly quiet. He would only chip in when something needed to be suggested or discussed. I was used to living frugally and having more money was not going to change this. However, I was breathing easier knowing that I didn't have to worry too much about my ability to cover expenses. I could allow myself a luxury here and there. I admit this would mostly be in the form of hiring an attractive and expensive female escort, treating them with costly dinner after which we would retire to a high-class hotel suite I'd booked for the night.

I was just having such a dinner with a pretty young lady by the name Lucy, when mother called me on my cell. Surprised, at first, I thought maybe I should not answer and let her leave me a message, but my curiosity prevailed. Apologizing to Lucy, I answered the phone.

"Yes?"

"Spinner, it's your mother."

"I know. Hi Mom, what's up?" I asked.

She was brief and to the point as usual.

"Listen, I was just cleaning grandma's room. My God, she had so much stuff in her closet. She never seemed to throw anything away… Anyway, going through all this I came across one manila envelope."

"Yeah? What's in it?" I asked, thinking – why was she telling me this?

"Well, it's sealed, and I didn't open it," my mother continued. "I respect her wishes. The envelope has your name on it. To which address would you like me to send it?

14

LUCY and LETTER

For some reason I was curious about the content of the envelope my grandmother left me. My first assumption was she'd left me money, and since I had enough, I asked my mother to open the envelope and keep any money that was inside.

She told me the envelope was thin, like nothing was inside. "No, it's not money," she said. "I think it's just a letter, and you should be the one reading it."

Well, all right then. I gave mother my P O Box address, which she already had but wasn't sure if I'd kept it after moving away from previous address.

The existence of that envelope made me a bit nervous, and I couldn't figure out why.

Charlie also found it necessary to give me his two cents worth. "This is worth checking out, Spinner," he let me know. "You never know what could hatch out of this."

Don't be so optimistic, although you might be right, I thought, but said nothing, not to freak out Lucy.

My grandmother probably only wanted to share with me her final goodbye. Some years ago, after my grandfather passed away, she moved in with my mother. I didn't see them frequently, because I maintained such poor contacts with Mom. My grandma was not religious like my mother although probably enough to be within her daughter's circle of tolerance. The first time I saw my grandmother was when my mother and I returned from Latvia after her unsuccessful attempt to talk my father into marrying her. I was around seven at the time.

Grandma Helen was nice to me and almost always took my side when I'd clashed with my mother. As I grew older, and became more rebellious, her fear increased that I might become a menace to society, and instead of finishing school and turning into a regular person, I would drift into an uncertain direction ... She read me well and figured out that I might be going down a different route than the path of an ordinary, law-abiding citizen.

I was puzzled. Why would she leave me a letter? We were never touchy-feely toward each other – same as my mother, and I must admit that being aloof kind of ran in our family.

I was thinking about all this while Lucy and I continued dining. Lucy noticed that I was somewhat absent and submerged into my thoughts.

"Is everything OK?" she asked me. "You look worried, my dear."

"Oh no, I'm fine," I rushed to convince her. "My grandmother passed away recently, and my mother just let me know that she found an envelope addressed to me."

"Sorry for your loss. But you might be getting some money," Lucy said. "This is how grandmothers are. My grandmother would buy me things, and when I became older, she would give me money to buy them myself."

My nervousness persisted, and I didn't feel that having company for the rest of the night would be very meaningful.

"Lucy," I said. "I hope you'll understand, but I feel a bit out of whack tonight. I don't know what it is, I'm just not quite myself. If you don't mind, I'd like to take off after dinner. You can spend the night in the hotel room I reserved or go home as you please. Of course, your reimbursement remains unchanged."

As I expected, Lucy had nothing against earning full honoraria, and not having to spend the night with me. She was raising her child as a single mother after splitting with the boy's father, and was cashing in on her good looks, looking forward to early retirement.

I had already made payment to her agency and gave her a huge tip which made her smile. I also suggested that the next time when I needed some company, I would ask specifically for her.

Next day, no letter. It took two more days for letter to finally arrive.

My mother had inserted the entire manila envelope from grandmother into a large postal envelope, without even folding it. She followed the 'do not bend' instruction handwritten on the front of the manila envelope. Other than this, there was only my name 'Spinner Walker' on it.

The envelope was thin, just as Mother said, and judging by examining it from the outside, it didn't seem to contain more but a sheet or two of paper. I grabbed the letter opener and carefully inserted it into one corner of the envelope and slowly cut the edge to gain access to its contents. I put the opener aside and split the top of the envelope, looking inside. I only saw two sheets of white paper, filled with densely written words in, I assumed, my grandmother's handwriting. I pulled out the paper and a small picture stashed between the sheets fell out.

I examined the picture first. It was an old black and white photograph, turning yellow from age, showing an older house. The house looked really old and in a bad shape. On the flip side of the picture there was nothing, no date, no description, nor an indication where this house was located. I finally turned my attention to the letter.

"Dear Spinner,

If everything goes as I planned, you will be reading this letter after my passing. Hopefully this will be many years from today. I feel I am in good health and see no reason why I wouldn't have a few more good years in front of me.

I decided not to share this with your mother – my daughter – out of shame, and because she is so preoccupied with her religious beliefs, she would not be interested in what I will say here.

If you are indeed reading this, it would mean that you are not jailed and hopefully have become a responsible person who remained on the right side of the law. I admit that, watching you grow up, I was worried you might turn out to be something else than I hoped for. I hope that by the time I die you will be a mature and decent adult that grew out of your early years of goofiness and have taken a positive direction in your life. As of now it looks to me you are still trying to figure out who you really are and what would be your role and position in life.

Although lately we haven't communicated much, you are the only possibly suitable person I have for this. And to tell you what 'this' is I must start by describing one episode in my life which took place back in the 1930s, when I was a young woman living with my parents in Oklahoma, in the house shown on the picture enclosed to this letter.

As a young person living in the rural, Indian Territory of remote Oklahoma prairie grassland, you could find yourself in pure wilderness if you step only a few minutes away from our house. At times I would do that myself, enjoying nature and fantasizing about a different life, as many young girls do. One day when I was out in the boonies, I heard a commotion and a human voice begging for help, coming from behind the bushes and a rock pile. I discovered there a seriously hurt young Indian man, laying on the ground, bleeding and looking exhausted. I had a flask with water on me and gave him some. I then ran back home and returned with food, and some towels. To make long story short, I fed him and cleaned the wounds, helping him to regain his strength. He quickly recovered, thanked me and took off, and I never saw him again. After a few weeks, when I was out in nature again, close to the same location where I found the wounded young Indian, I saw another man on a horse. He was much older and dressed in a beautiful traditional Indian outfit. He approached me and began talking. He was the local Indian tribe chief, and the young man I helped earlier was his younger son. His son told him that I saved his life, and the chief wanted to thank me. He then told me what had happened to his son who also had a brother. The older son went hunting, and two days later his wife approached the younger son and propositioned him. When the young man refused out of respect for his brother, she pushed him into a hole in the ground and left him there to die. The young man struggled for a full day and night before he was able to dig himself out of that hole. He was disoriented, hurt and exhausted and couldn't find his way back to the village. This was when I found him. With my help he recovered and returned to his village and told his father and brother what have happened to him. To punish the rotten woman, they cut her hair off, stripped her of her clothes and forced her into the same hole in the ground where she pushed his younger son. She was unable to free herself from the hole and eventually died from thirst. The old man was looking for me to thank me for what I had done. He brought me a gift, which he had inherited from his own grandfather. It was the gift 'one was supposed to pass to the person better than they were.' The gift had two components. One was incredibly valuable to white people, and another, deeply sacred and enchanted to the Indians. He handed me these gifts which were wrapped in a beautifully decorated Indian fabric.

I thanked him and took the package and hid it in our house. At that time my father was in the process of adding a bathroom to the house and I noticed a loose wall panel under the bathroom sink. I hid the package there.

Many years later I returned and added a note to the package, which you can read if you retrieve the gifts.

I hope, my only grandson, you will be a better person than I am, and more deserving of these gifts. Eventually you might find someone even better to pass it on to. But you are free to use them any way you feel appropriate.

The address where I hid the package is 439 Evening Rose in Whitewell, Oklahoma.

I hope you will find in your heart forgiveness when you read the note I left there.

Although I was never able to show this to you properly, I love you very much.

Your grandmother Helen."

Whoa.

Yes, I was intrigued. Of course, I wanted to go to Oklahoma. Greedy Charlie was also all for it, too. He smelled more money. No, I had nothing better to do. Grandma left me with more questions than answers.

Out of habit I visited the library to check the map of the place where I was supposed to go.

I found out two facts, one more disturbing than the other. First, Whitewell was close to the border with Kansas, and that reminded me of Petra and everything else that had recently happened to me. And second, on the map of Whitewell there was no street named Evening Rose.

15

MARGIE and CLARA

Welcome to Whitewell! I drove in from Oklahoma City through Interstate 35, and State Hwy 11 in a black BMW rented at Will Rogers Airport. I arrived via Chicago, because there was no direct flight from New York. Bummer! It was almost 5 p.m. when I reached my destination and I was exhausted. I checked in at the Holiday Inn Express and after dinner went to my room.

I had no idea why there was no Evening Rose street in Whitewell, but I had a plan on how to proceed. I didn't want to think that the house might have been demolished. No sirree Bob! Got to stay positive! What I didn't have, was a plan how to execute the retrieval of the package after the house was located. The options included burglarizing the house when the occupants were absent and steal the Indian gifts. Or, I could pretend to be a plumber, knock on the door and make up a story that would let me into the house's bathroom, and that way get to the goodies. Another possible option was to visit the house occupants and honestly tell them that I was the grandson of a woman who used to live there and hope the current tenants would be hospitable enough to let me snoop around and use the restroom where the valuables were hidden.

Each option carried a great deal of risk and uncertainty. I hated that. The problem was that no matter which option was chosen I would likely have only one shot at it.

Charlie was talkative during the trip, speculating what the 'gifts' could be. His focus was on the part described by grandmother as 'incredibly valuable to white people.' His initial guess that it could be gold was soon dismissed, because gold, to be 'incredibly valuable' would be too heavy and impractical for handling. Grandma never mentioned anything about the package being weighty. His next guess were diamonds. There could be one single gigantic diamond worth millions. If this was the case, he suggested I should auction it off, and move away, where we could live in paradise, drinking margaritas and having fun.

I was more realistic and wondered why the grandmother never cashed out this 'incredibly valuable item to white people.' And, what could be the Indian portion of the gift; described as 'sacred and enchanted?' No idea. Grandma's self-description that she was a bad person worried me. What did she do to ask for my forgiveness, and why did she choose me to pass on these gifts? Finally, why was she ashamed to share the story and wealth with my mother?

This was puzzling. With a nice chunk of cash already in my account, I was less concerned about the potential value of the gifts. However, I had to admit that Charlie's greed was actually my own and it was me subconsciously thinking about how this was a chance to obtain additional wealth.

The fact that I had no idea where grandma's house was didn't concern me too much. I had a plan! This was the first order of business – to locate the damn house.

First thing the next morning I stopped at the local hardware store and purchased items which I believed would help me remove the panel hiding the gifts. I bought two sets of flathead and Phillips screwdrivers, a crowbar and hammer. I added the tools to a plastic bag in which I already had a t-shirt, to be switched with the package.

Whitewell was a small city with a population of less than ten thousand, and I figured that driving through town I might recognize the house from the picture grandma provided. After an hour of riding, I realized that this was not working well. Too many streets, not enough patience.

Charlie wasn't helpful in this, and I was glad to see that my planning and figuring out what to do was better than Charlie's. I sensed that he was a bit jealous to my superiority.

"What shall we do, Spinner," he asked. "To find the house the way you're trying is like looking for a needle in a haystack."

"Do you have better idea?" I asked.

"Not really," he admitted.

"Then quit nagging, and you'll see," I said, feeling condescending.

Going through the brochure rack back in the hotel's lobby, I saw one advertising the local library, and the library was the place where I knew I should start.

This is what I did. Went right to the reference desk, and by clearing my throat addressed the woman sitting behind it.

"May I help you?" she said, raising her head.

"I hope so," I answered. "I'm not a local and I am trying to find a house in which my grandmother used to live. I am looking for Evening Rose street, but the map lists no street by that name. Can you help me?"

She nodded and turned to her computer. "Evening Rose, you say?" She started working her computer and after a while she confirmed, "you're right, there is no street by that name in Whitewell.

"Well, what should I do?" I asked.

"And you're sure this was the Whitewell address?"

"Positive."

I showed her the picture of the house hoping she might recognize it, but she shook her head 'no.' She paused a bit, and then suggested, "Maybe Margie, our volunteer could help. She is an old-timer and knows everything about Whitewell. She will be here later today. Could you come back at three?"

I wasn't too crazy of waiting that long and doing nothing.

"Well, I don't plan to hang around much longer. Would it be possible to contact that lady and ask her over the phone?"

To my surprise, she agreed. "I'll be glad to!"

And she called Margie, who didn't have the answer firsthand but suggested that I should contact the City of Whitewell Street Department and ask to see Chuck. She even had the address and before long I was facing overweight Chuck who turned out to be polite and helpful.

"I'm not surprised," he said. "For some reason they changed several street names back in the Sixties and Seventies. Luckily, there is a record of these changes and if you give me few minutes, I'll get them for you."

And he left the room. When he returned, he was smiling. "Got it! It's only few minutes from here. Your street is now called Oklahoma Avenue. Just continue down the road and turn right to 177. Then turn left on Oklahoma and look for your number. You can't miss it."

Thanks, Chuck! Back in the car, I hoped maybe my luck would continue. I was positive and stayed vertical. I drove off as per his instructions and in less than ten minutes I was parked across the street from the house I was looking for. Yep, this was the house – it looked the same as in the photograph.

I observed the house, figuring out my next step. My curiosity increased, and I decided to press my luck. I left my footprints everywhere. I inquired about that address at the library and city streets department. It would be stupid to do anything illegal. I got out of the car and approached the house.

"What are you doing?" Charlie asked. I heard a touch of panic in his normally flat voice.

"I'm going in, Charlie," I said and approached the front door.

"This might be premature, Spinner," he continued. "It would be better to think it over and prepare."

"What the hell, I feel lucky today," I said and knocked on the door.

It didn't take long for the door to open, and an old, skinny lady showed up.

"Hello, may I help you?"

I quickly assessed the situation. Judging by the look on the old lady's face and her tone of voice she had no fear of me whatsoever.

"I am awfully sorry to disturb you, Ma'am. My name is Spinner and I stopped here because my grandmother used to live here. She recently passed away in Chicago, and I was just curious…"

"Oh, how nice of you to be interested in your grandma's homestead. Sorry for your loss."

"Thank you. You see, she left me a picture of the house," I said pulling out the picture and showing it to the old lady.

"I see," she said, and continued: "You are welcome to come inside."

This was unbelievably easy. The old lady must have spent her entire life there, as a part of this small, still unspoiled community, where the trust between people remained present in their everyday lives. Her age also contributed to such trust.

"Thank you, this is so nice of you, I wouldn't mind," I said and entered the house.

The interior of the house was modest and in poor condition. The lady said to call her Clara, and took me around the house, which was messy and compartmented into two tiny bedrooms, a small living room and a kitchen. And, most importantly, the bathroom.

She offered me to sit on a couch and we talked about how long she'd been living in the house, about her family and her life in Whitewell, and so forth. She remembered a bit about my grandma and her family and told me some details about them. I reciprocated and told her all I knew about my grandmother. Clara was a widow and lived alone with a cat who came right to me, rubbing herself against my elbow. My own cat was less affectionate toward me than this one, perhaps only reflecting the trait of her owner.

Clara offered me coffee and I said that a glass of water would do. When she went to the kitchen I asked if I could use the bathroom.

"Of course," Clara said. "Pardon the mess, I didn't expect visitors."

I entered, taking my plastic bag, and sat on the toilet because the sink was very close to it. I began working on a panel below the sink. Although nervous and not much good with my hands, I managed to remove the panel right away because it was so loose that it was a miracle it didn't fall off by itself.

My heart was pounding faster when I saw a meticulously decorated cloth wrapped over something of a size smaller than I expected. Two rubber bands were securing the content. I removed the package and pulled out the t-shirt from my bag, placing it in the hole in the wall. The package replaced the t-shirt at the bottom of my plastic bag. I then tried to attach the panel back to cover the opening in the wall, but it kept falling out. I looked around and spotted a roll of duct tape on the top of the washer. I quickly removed a piece and taped the panel somehow in place where it was supposed to be.

Before exiting I flushed the toilet and washed my hands. Clara was sitting on the couch and flipping through the pages of a photo album.

"Here you are," she said. "I have some old pictures here; with some people I don't even recognize. Take a look."

I sat next to Clara and browsed through the album pages. There was one photo showing a smiling young lady, which looked familiar to me.

"I'm not a hundred percent sure, but this could be my grandmother."

Clara flipped the photo over and asked: "I thought so. What did you say her name was?"

"Helen," I said, and Clara's face shined in a big smile.

"There! It says Helen, Agnes and Greg!" she pointed triumphantly. I looked at my young grandmother and realized the picture was also dated: July 7, 1948. Wow!

Naturally I was looking forward to bringing my visit to an end. I said that I should be going and pulled out from my pocked two 50-dollar bills and gave it to her.

"Please take this as my appreciation for your kindness and time. It was so nice meeting you, Clara."

The old lady accepted my money with tears in her eyes. She must have been quite destitute.

"You don't have to do this," she said. "But thank you, thank you so much!" And she invited me to come and visit any time in the future.

I drove a few blocks and parked my car, eager to see what was wrapped in the cloth. I carefully removed the rubber bands and unwrapped the fabric. Inside was a folded piece of paper – my grandmother's note, and two individually fabric-wrapped pieces, each tied with twine. I carefully untied the larger and heavier one. It was a leather pouch and inside the pouch were about two dozen coins. I knew nothing about coins. I only knew some coins could be valuable. I carefully unwrapped the other piece and found an Indian necklace. The necklace appeared old and therefore could be valuable. I knew that both gifts could be expensive, although I personally would not pay much to obtain them. I didn't really know what I should expect, but the pieces I found left me mildly disappointed. I knew this was rather stupid of me – what else could be in the package that would leave me more excited?

I hoped reading my grandmother's note would better explain the 'incredible value' of these pieces. I decided to read my grandmother's note back in the comfort of my hotel room.

16
INDIAN and TILLY

"Whoever is reading this note – and I hope it will be my grandson – is now a designated keeper of the gifts enclosed here. To deserve these gifts, the individual selected as a designated keeper should be a better person than the person passing them.

The objects enclosed here were given to me by an old Indian chief who thanked me for saving his son. He described the circumstances under which he acquired them. One is a bag containing coins, which the Indian chief received from his grandfather. When this grandfather was a young man, he captured a white man he named Big Nose, trespassing through territory that belonged to the Indian tribe. Big Nose begged for his life, and in exchange offered the coin collection he carried, which he described as very valuable to the white people. The grandfather pretended to agree, took the coins and let the man go. He also asked Big Nose to examine the necklace, which is also enclosed, asking if the white man thought the necklace was valuable. Big Nose didn't think so and took off. The Indian never intended to let the white man free, but to use this opportunity to practice following the enemy with the purpose of eventually killing him in a cruel predator-prey game. There was a storm that night and Big Nose took shelter under a tree, which was hit by lightning, and killing him in an instant.

I was curious how much were the coins worth and took them to a coin appraiser who confirmed that the collection had some very rare coins and estimated they all could easily be worth several thousand dollars, with the value increasing over time.

The old Indian chief said that Big Nose died because he touched the necklace while not being its designated keeper. When the grandfather passed the gifts on to his grandson, the Indian chief rubbed the necklace, described as sacred and enchanted, against his older son's wife, who was 'rotten.' She was then forced into a hole in the ground. Eventually they found her remains; she had died from thirst and was partially eaten by wild animals. This convinced the chief that the necklace was really magical.

I took the necklace to a reputable retailer of Indian jewelry who became very excited examining it, not because he identified the necklace but because he couldn't. The necklace had a part he recognized as some kind of fetish or amulet, distantly resembling something he called African juju. He said the necklace was likely not made by the Indians, but he had never seen anything like it. He took pictures of the necklace to do further research. I returned the next day and discovered that his store had been destroyed in a fire and he had perished with it.

I became uneasy about all this. What if there was some truth to the story of the old Indian chief about the necklace being bewitched. But I was still skeptical.

It will be difficult writing the rest of this note, but I have to confess. At one time I discovered that my husband was having an affair. I found him in my own bed with his young lover. I was beside myself, enraged and screaming. I grabbed the Indian necklace from my drawer and threw it at them shouting 'would you like to take my jewelry too?' The necklace hit the young woman in the face and my husband picked it up and threw it back at me. I was hoping what I heard about the necklace was true and they would die. What can I say? They both died shortly thereafter in terrible accidents and it would pain me too much to go into the details. But now I do believe the legend about neckless being enchanted is correct. From that moment on I have carried the terrible burden of feeling guilty, being a never-caught murderer. I regret and I am ashamed what I have done. I know that my unfaithful husband and his girlfriend didn't deserve to die. I should have either forgiven him or divorced him.

Feeling more and more guilt, I decided to return the Indian gifts back behind the wall under the bathroom sink in the Whitewell house where I grew up, and eventually pass it to someone who is a better person than me.

I hope the soul reading this note will indeed be a better one than I am. This person is now a designated keeper and will not be harmed by touching or wearing the necklace. I am still not sure if all deaths related to this necklace were just weird coincidences or the necklace really does possess some mystical powers. All I can say is – please be very careful, I wish you good luck, and please, please, forgive me for what I've done.

Helen P."

I was reading this note with my mouth open. First, you were forgiven, grandma. No wonder you didn't want to share this with my mother. Second – what the hell? I had no words to describe my feelings. I was laying in my hotel bed trying to process what I'd just read. Charlie was also excited, focusing on the coins. "This is great! You don't need to sell the coins right away," he suggested. "You have enough money for now, and with the passage of time coins like these will only gaining value. You are a rich man now, Spinner, you are set for life!"

Money. Didn't Joe once tell me money wasn't everything? I didn't believe him, but at the moment I was more focused on that necklace. Was everything I'd read really possible? I unwrapped the necklace again, avoided touching it and I looked at it as if it would kill me on contact. But I hoped I'd be safe – I was a designated keeper. My grandma Helen had her doubts about the necklace, and so did I. Was it possible that the damn necklace was really somehow bewitched? Despite not being superstitious I couldn't eliminate the facts that there were things in the world we humans had not yet been able to understand and explain. And some of them we probably never would. Grandma also suspected this but wasn't sure. Just in case, I should better be damn careful with the necklace. I couldn't see what use I would have from it. I would have to think about that. I scrutinized the necklace again. To me it looked ordinary, old and even kind of ugly. Being no jewelry expert, I would have a hard time even describing it. It was a combination of green and brown colors, very dark, almost black, matte and dull. Sinister. On the end was hanging that charm, or should I say hex. It was an irregularly shaped, semitransparent stone or some other type of material, and resembled nothing familiar – animal or any other object – it only had an abstract sign etched in the middle of it, and it was inside of it, and not on its surface like one would expect.

I was tired but not hungry. The hotel had no room service and I would have to go out for dinner. It was getting late and I decided I would spend one more night in the hotel, to get a good rest.

To get my mind off my grandmother's note, I turned on the TV and began flipping through channels, looking for some old movie or similar kind of entertainment. One channel was in the middle of broadcasting the news which caught my attention. There was an outbreak of an unknown illness in a government research facility, which took the life of three women and put five more in the hospital where they were fighting for their lives. All this sounded familiar, and I found another channel with more detailed news. I learned they were talking about the infamous Federal Animal Disorder Research

Center of Hopkins in Kansas. They were talking about the Mr. Laos' operation that was moved from Duke of Prunes Island to Kansas.

It was like somebody poked me with a needle in my rear end and I jumped from my bed. What the hell? Was this a 'here we go again' moment or what? I switched channels looking for more news and saw that everybody was talking about it. This was no setup like in Mrs. Miller's basement.

What was happening there? Petra immediately came to mind. Was she infected? Was she OK? And Lydia, the woman who tried to stop Lutz by setting him and his germs on fire. Was she alive? I don't know why, but I thought I should be informed about this firsthand.

"This is not your business, Spinner," Charlie said, guessing what I was thinking.

"I need to see if Petra is OK, right?" I still knew Petra's cell number.

As I reached for the phone, Charlie said: "All right, if you insist. But perhaps you should try to locate Tilly first."

I put my phone down. Who the hell was Tilly? And why in the world should I locate her?

"Why?" I automatically asked.

I detected a dash of triumph in Charlie's voice when he answered: "I'll explain."

17

BRUCE and OKLAHOMA

"You know what," I said, "I'm sorry, but whatever it is, it'll have to wait. First I want to know what's going on with Petra."

"As you wish," Charlie agreed.

So, I called Petra's number. It didn't connect right away. It was the first time I'd tried to reach her after we split. I respected her decision to leave me, although I was still in a state of shock and longing for her. I hated myself for not putting up at least some effort to try saving our relationship. I did nothing because I knew it was over, not only from what she said but also from the way she said it. Ever since Charlie had awakened in me and Petra became aware of my alter ego, she began withdrawing and distancing herself more and more.

After the fourth ring, she picked up the call. She answered, and she knew it was me! She kept my name and number in her phone contact list.

I apologized for bothering her, but because of the TV news I wanted to check up on her and confirm that she was all right.

She didn't seem upset with me nor complained that I called, but she sounded weak. The news was not good. She was one of five women that were in the hospital, diagnosed with an unknown disease that was, in a peculiar way, targeting only women. They would suffer from severe dehydration and to keep them hydrated they had to be continuously fed through an IV. The rapid progression of the illness was fatal to some, and Lydia was one who didn't make it. Mr. Laos' daughter, Elizabeth, was also infected and he quickly transported her to a private hospital in Hong Kong.

"What about you? What hospital are you in?" I asked.

"Local," she said. "I'm in quarantine. They won't let my parents see me because I'm contagious. I apparently infected one nurse here."

"What can I do to help?" I asked.

"I don't know," she quietly said. "Thanks for calling, Spinner. I've got to go."

"Go where?" I asked, but she had already disconnected.

I was puzzled and the conversation upset me. What the hell was going on here? I didn't know where the 'local' hospital was located. I should have asked. And that bastard, Mr. Laos, took his daughter to Hong Kong and left his girlfriend in that 'local' hospital. Pretty shitty, if you ask me.

"Are you ready now to get in touch with Tilly?" Charlie asked.

"Is that all you have to say? Charlie, now you're pissing me off," I said. "I'm not in the mood for your bullshit. Don't you see how upset I am? I have no idea what's going on. Petra might die, she acted strangely, you heard her. I don't know why her billionaire boyfriend moved his daughter to Hong Kong, but left Petra behind. Where the hell is the hospital where Petra is? With all this, you keep bothering me with this damn bloody Tilly."

"If you'd only listen to me for a minute, Spinner. Don't be so stubborn. I deserve a little benefit of the doubt. Give me a chance to explain and you'll see that I'm not changing the subject," Charlie said rapidly.

"Speak," I said.

"Thank you. When Lydia and Lutz engaged in a pissing match, screaming at each other at the top of their lungs, your adrenaline skyrocketed, and you became extremely excited. In the commotion you apparently missed some details. But your memory keeps everything you ever saw or heard. Only, you can't access all 100 percent of it, but I can. So, when they were screaming, name-calling, and insulting each other, Lutz shouted that he regretted providing that bitch Tilly with the medicine that would save her from his revenge. In your earlier conversation with Max, he mentioned Lutz's girlfriend, and her name, Mathilda. Tilly is a nickname for Mathilda. Putting two and two together, I think that Tilly has the pills or something that can cure this disease Petra has. Lutz mentioned that she moved to Oklahoma to be with her sister. I told you this was not your business, but you wanted to get involved. Well, you might want to try locating Tilly, and ask her to share the medicine, give a dose to Petra and the rest to the authorities. They can go into mass production of the medicine and solve the problem quickly. You would be a hero who saved the world's females. That's all."

I was stunned not only because of what he said, but also because I didn't remember almost any of it. And yet, all this sounded familiar. Gee, it looked like having Charlie as my helper was not such a bad thing after all. Crazy Lutz wasn't so crazy, and he created the remedy for the germs he designed. He must have loved his girlfriend otherwise he wouldn't give her the medication. Of course, we had to locate Tilly, and save Petra, if not the world.

I knew this would be easier said than done. Going to the library again and expecting that some Margie or Chuck would supply the information needed wouldn't cut it. No, this was a job for the professionals.

I searched the Internet and after much consideration selected *Yappa Investigations* from Tulsa. They were the largest, oldest and presumably the best such agency in the region. I gave them a call and soon I was speaking to their principal agent, Bruce Santini.

Yes, he said, they could be hired over the phone. They were doing that all the time. What was the problem? To find a person? No problem! Did I have a credit card? Yes.

"What is the name of the person you wish to find?" Bruce asked.

"Mathilda. She also goes by Tilly," I said.

"Mathilda what?" he inquired.

"Don't really know," I said, expecting his whining to begin.

"Don't have her last name?"

"Correct."

"You have her picture?"

"Nope."

"You have her description? Physical attributes?" He surprised me, continuing questioning, and not complaining.

"Afraid not."

"How old is she?"

"Couldn't tell you."

"What is her location?"

"It could be anywhere in the state of Oklahoma."

I expected Bruce would say something like 'is this a joke?' but instead he asked: "All right, what other information about that person you do have?"

"Well, she used to work at a facility that was located on Duke of Prunes Island. All I know is that she moved to Oklahoma to be with her sister. I know nothing about her sister. Mathilda was single as far as I know, and all this happened a few months ago, just at the time when Duke of Prunes was closed down and relocated to Kansas."

Bruce didn't seem to be discouraged with so poor quality of information he was given.

"Our regular hourly rate is $150 plus expenses. For cases without sufficient information we charge a special rate of $180 per hour. If you don't receive useful results you still agree to pay us 25 percent for the hours spent on your case and cover accrued expenses."

"That's fine. My time is of the essence. I need results super-fast, and I am willing to pay extra."

"I can put my best investigators on the case right away. You will have results by the end of the business day tomorrow or sooner. The hourly rate for urgent special cases is $220."

"Sure."

"What is the top amount you would let us spend for extra expenses?"

"What kind of expenses are we talking here?" I asked.

"You know, we have certain connections at certain places, but we have to pay them for information they provide. We will obtain the list of employees at Duke of Prunes, credit card usages, phone record reports, drivers record and similar."

"I see. Well, don't go over five thousand without calling me first," I said.

"I don't expect we will come even close to this amount."

"Wonderful. I'll tip you an extra $500 if you find that person."

"All right, then," Bruce said. "Now I will need the information from your credit card."

After our conversation was over, Charlie commented: "I like this guy. I think he is professional and will do good job."

"Let's hope so," I said nervously. I wondered why Petra abruptly ended my phone call, and I wanted to let her know that I was working to bringing her a remedy for the illness. I dialed her number again.

After three rings I heard the characteristic three-tone beeps and the robotic female voice: "The number you have dialed has been disconnected. There is no forwarding information available."

18

KEITH and REMEDY

The next day, by 5:30 p.m. I was already en route to Oklahoma City. I had on me Tilly's address, her full name and picture. She looked a bit older than me, and her facial features were forgettable. Bruce and his team did well. The charge for the whole shebang came to almost $2,000, but I didn't complain because I got the information I wanted. Bruce cautioned me that Tilly's address was in a district with the highest car insurance premiums in the city. Tilly's sister had died, and Tilly was currently sharing her sister's apartment with her boyfriend. Neither one of them worked and they were living off the proceeds from the sale of Tilly's sister's personal possessions. Bruce added that the couple frequented a nearby bar called *Waterhole Island*.

"This might be good," said Charlie. "If you offer to buy the medicine from her, she will probably go for it, because she needs money. Just don't be too generous and make her think that you are loaded."

It took me two hours to reach my destination and I went straight to a nearby motel I'd found through the GPS built into the car. The neighborhood appearance confirmed Bruce's report. The buildings in the area appeared deteriorated and neglected, and the streets were dirty and desolate. I chose a lodging nearest to Tilly's address. The motel room I booked was very basic and not very clean. I couldn't see any bugs or spiders, but the carpet was suspiciously stained, and the bed comforter was old and discolored.

"You don't want to leave valuables in this room when you are not around, Spinner," Charlie commented.

I agreed that the coin collection and the necklace shouldn't be left in that room unattended. I didn't want to spend much time hanging around, and I soon drove off to the address at Warr Acres, where Tilly resided. Her one-story apartment complex looked like it had been converted from an old motel and was falling apart. I found the door, 22B, and knocked. No answer. I pressed my ear against the door but there was no sound to be heard.

"She's probably in the saloon," Charlie speculated.

"I know," I said. It was dark, and I searched the GPS for Waterhole Island. The joint was just straight down the road about a mile and a half away.

The bar was in the middle of a large, empty area and indeed resembled a waterhole in the Sahara Desert. Distant and rusty metal buildings – perhaps warehouses and small factory shops could be seen in the distance. The front of the saloon was poorly lit, with a parking area occupied with a few cars and motorcycles. The building was a wooden structure that must have been built in the 19th century and since never maintained. One small tree on each side of the bar framed the building.

I didn't feel confident when entering and I had no real plan how to proceed. Instead I would have to play it by ear. Inside was a surprisingly decent-looking sports bar, with a dimly lit room, and a richly carved vintage bar counter stretching from one side of the room to the other; with matching bar stools in front, and a few tables

111

on the side, and the heavy smell of cigarette smoke. Yes, smoking was permitted, and judging by the substantial amount of smoke in the air – encouraged. Two pool tables, a pinball machine and two different game machines were in the corner, with a dartboard on the wall. Few patrons were in the room and paid no attention to my entering. A small, empty stage, with music coming from the speakers, and a couple of large hanging TV screens: one showing a football match, and another one a bowhunting show.

Only one person was playing pool. I instantly recognized Tilly. She was alone, and I approached her. She was taller and skinnier than she looked in her picture. Her hair was straight, touching her shoulders and partially covered her face.

"Pardon me, are you Tilly?" I said.

She turned and measured me up with her eyes.

"Maybe," she answered. "Who wants to know?"

"My name is Spinner," I said. "Mr. Laos from Duke of Prunes sent me, asking if you would let me have the pills Lutz gave you. They could quickly make more medicine needed to take care of the outbreak." I thought such a direct approach could be the most effective.

She stared for a moment, as if processing what she had just heard. She looked intoxicated, either with alcohol or drugs.

"Lutz didn't give me any pills, pal," she mumbled. "What the hell are you talking about?"

"I can pay you," I said quickly. "You can give me only half of what you got and keep the rest for yourself if you need it."

"Why would I need these pills?"

"Didn't you see on TV? There was an outbreak of illness. I don't know how bad it is, but you have the medicine for it, from Lutz."

"I don't watch TV. Lutz didn't give me no pills. He gave me a bottle with liquid. I should take a teaspoon for ten days if I need it. I took one spoon. It tasted awful. It didn't do nothing for me."

"That's what I'm talking about! If you let me have half of the bottle, I'll give you 500 for it," I said, excited.

Our conversation was interrupted. "Is this Bozo bothering you, babe?" I heard a voice behind me and turned around. There was a big, athletic guy, with long hair and a beard, wearing a short sleeved black leather jacket. He looked threatening and obviously ready to kick the shit out of me, and he had a nasty odor. The whole situation was rapidly becoming more unpleasant.

"Easy, Keith. This guy wants me to sell him the medicine from Lutz," she quickly said.

He paused, still looking at me suspiciously, as if he was itching to hit me. He was undecided.

"Really? How much?" he finally asked.

"I am offering $500 for half a bottle," I said, hoping their greed would prevail and they would go for it. Keith was also drunk, but I hoped not so drunk that he wouldn't smell a good deal.

"How about a thousand?" he said.

A counteroffer! "I'll give you 600," I said, ready to bargain.

"One thousand," he repeated.

I evaluated the situation. This guy was not to be trusted. Tilly was not to be trusted. Neither one was rational, nor sober. I was unsure what would be the best way to proceed. If I agreed to $1,000, he might ask for two. But they were willing to sell. They wanted money and didn't think they needed the medicine.

"750," I said, "this is my final offer. Take it or leave it."

He was looking right at me, trying to read me. So, I completed my offer: "I'll have the money here tomorrow morning, say, around eleven. Come, bring the stuff and we'll do business."

I thought maybe by that time they would sober up and I would be able to explain the situation. Ultimately, I would give them a thousand.

To my surprise Keith agreed, but Tilly didn't. "Keith!" she said and nudged him in a rib with her elbow.

"Tomorrow. One thousand. I'll meet you in front of the bar. Make it noon." And he turned to Tilly. "Let's go, babe."

I nodded, but Keith didn't even look at me. Despite Tilly's protesting, he pushed her out of the bar.

I wasn't sure what to think. I ordered a beer. I didn't look forward to going back to my motel room. The saloon was actually pleasant. I didn't have as much cash as this guy wanted. I would have to go to the bank and take more cash out. I hated that I had to spend the night here and thought I could try finding another, more decent hotel room.

I exited the bar, and the fresh air felt good on my skin. I walked toward where my car was parked, when something whacked me from behind. The blow on my head caused me to hit the ground and knocked me unconscious.

I don't know how long it took before I regained my awareness. The back of my head was bloody. I got up and tried to stop the bleeding by pressing my wound with the paper tissue I pulled from my pocket. I was trying to clear my thoughts and figure out what just happened.

"It was Keith who hit you," Charlie said. "Are you going to be OK?"

"I'll be fine," I said and checked my pockets. My wallet with cash, credit card and driver's license were gone. I saw my BMW was still there. I hoped the coins I left in the car were still there. My car keys? I checked my pockets again, but they were gone too. Strangely, they didn't take the car. The Indian necklace I carried in my pocket was also gone. So was my phone and the key to my motel room. They cleaned me out good.

I looked around. There I was in the middle of the night, in the middle of the nowhere, with no ID, and no money. I couldn't enter my car, couldn't call anybody, and I was bleeding from the back of my head. But I was determined to take care of business, get back my possessions and all that without involving the police.

19

REBECCA and HOPKINS

"What now?" Charlie said.

"Back to the motel."

I took off walking in the direction of my motel. I remembered: it was just up the road. Charlie could also help, need be, with directions. The walk was unpleasant. It was dark, cold, uneven and long. I was used to driving everywhere and a mile and a half on foot felt like five. My head was still hurting but the bleeding had stopped. I had to pay careful attention to every step I took. This slowed me down, and after tripping few more times I realized it was better to be slow and safe than risk another fall rushing.

It must have been very late when I finally came to my motel. I knocked on the lobby's locked door and a heavy-set woman anywhere between 25 and 60 years old, with the nametag 'Rebecca' attached to her blouse, came closer, distrustfully observing me through the glass. I must have looked a bit unusual.

"May I help you?" were her words, actually meaning 'what the hell do you want?'

"Good evening, Ma'am," I said, trying to sound polite and honest. "Yes, I'm a guest here, and I had a little accident. I lost my car keys. My room key, phone and documents are all locked in my car."

"What is your name?" she asked.

"Spinner Walker," I said, watching her duck-walking back to the reception counter.

She returned wearing a bit more friendly face.

"What happened?" she asked, still not unlocking the door.

"I had one drink too many at the Waterhole saloon. I fell, holding the car keys in my hand. I dropped them, and I couldn't find them because it was too dark."

She seemed to be satisfied with my story and unlocked the door.

"You don't look well. My God, is that blood on your shoulder? Do you want me to call an ambulance?"

No, no. I elaborated that I had stepped on something, twisted my ankle and fell down, back first, and must have hit a rock or something. All I needed was to take a shower, clean myself up and rest. In the morning I intended to go back and get my keys. No need to panic.

"All right. I hope your wound won't get infected." And Rebecca, bless her heart, handed me the spare key to my room. "Nothing happens without a reason. Maybe this was God's way of preventing you driving your car drunk. You never know."

"Very true. Thanks, Rebecca. I appreciate your understanding. Good night."

I was so grateful that I had booked my room when I first arrived in town. I took a shower, dried myself and changed my clothes.

"What's the plan?" Charlie asked.

"First thing in the morning I'm gonna pay them a surprise visit. That's the plan," I said.

"Spinner, this could be dangerous. This Keith guy is crazy. He might panic. You don't know if you can negotiate with him, or if he's going to punch you."

"They don't know I have their address," I said.

"So what? You couldn't protect yourself, if that guy attacks you. He is stronger than you. You should at least give Rebecca a letter and tell her to call the police if she doesn't hear from you by certain time."

"And in the letter, I can tell the police 'hi there, please hurry, here is the address where you will find my dead body? It was Keith who did it.' This is poor consolation, Charlie."

"I know. That's why I didn't think this was a good idea in the first place."

"What else can I do, Charlie? I have no ID, can't get in my car, my phone is gone. You think I should go to the police?"

"It might not be such a bad idea. You didn't do anything wrong. You were robbed, and you know who the perpetrators are. You can take the police to where your things are."

"Yeah but in that case, I will have no chance to get that damn medicine. I've already invested so much into it. I need to try. I'm counting on the element of surprise. I can use your idea about that letter. I will tell them a taxi is waiting for me and if I don't return in ten minutes, the driver will take my letter to the police. In the letter I listed their names, address, a description of what they've done. This should prevent them of hurting me, I hope."

"Your plan is risky, and I know you are trying to avoid risk. How will you pay for a taxi?"

"I am not taking a taxi, I will only tell them that I did, but I'll walk there."

"I guess it doesn't make any difference. Your bluff might work. Offer him more money for the medicine and for the return of your possessions. This would amount to more cash than they got from your wallet. Tell them you won't press any charges."

Right. Now, you're talking, Charlie.

I removed the comforter from the bed and laid down dressed, on top of the sheets, to rest. I was tired and even fell asleep for a while, waking up around seven in the morning.

117

"Time to go, Charlie."

And I took off on foot, letting Charlie guide me to Tilly's apartment. Luckily the apartment was only walking distance from the motel. The crisp morning air was clearing my head but chilling my body and when I arrived at Tilly's place, I was pretty stiff.

Without hesitating I knocked on door 22B. I supposed they were still in bed. I knocked again, harder, and took a few steps back from the door. Nothing. I gave them another minute and then knocked on the door even harder. Again, nothing.

I put my ear against the door and no sound could be heard from inside. I automatically grabbed the doorknob and turned it. To my surprise the door was not locked, and I slowly pushed it open.

The curtains over the room windows were heavy, preventing daylight from entering the room. The light in the room was on. I saw both, Tilly and Keith, lying motionless on the floor near the kitchen table. The room was in disarray. One chair was knocked over, and another one was pushed against the wall. I entered, realizing there was no immediate danger. I shut the door behind me and approached them. They must have passed out drunk, celebrating their steal. When I came closer, I deduced neither one of them was breathing. I checked them out and finally concluded both of them were dead.

This naturally raised my adrenaline level. I assessed the situation. There was an open bottle of vodka, and pills on the table. Both of them must have overdosed. Probably overjoyed with the success of their crime, they were celebrating and overdosed. My wallet was on the kitchen table, nothing missing but my cash. Everything else was also there, my car keys, and the Indian necklace, plus the motel key and my phone.

Oh shit – the necklace! It was the necklace that killed them! I picked up my possessions and put them in my pockets. Charlie must have realized that I had become erratic.

"C'mon, Spinner, you don't believe that necklace has anything to do with this?"

I hoped so, but I didn't know what to believe. I wasn't superstitious, but with two dead people on the floor, and the grandmother's stories about the necklace, I was becoming confused. Was I a killer? Or was it all just a freaky coincidence?

"You didn't do anything wrong, Spinner," Charlie started his tirade. "You didn't push the necklace on them. They took it from you. Even if the necklace is cursed, their deaths are not on you. It was their stupidity and greed that killed them. You were robbed and they were celebrating what they did, and simply overdosed. The necklace has nothing to do with it. Don't feel guilty and don't waste time on dwelling on this. You're clean as a whistle. Find the medicine and get the hell out of here. Don't leave any fingerprints. Avoid complications."

Charlie was right. It was so good to have him. I started snooping around making sure not to touch anything. The bathroom was the place to start. It was small, dirty and crowded with bathroom paraphernalia. Above the sink was a small cabinet behind the mirror. I tore down some sheets of toilet paper, wrapped them around my hand and opened the cabinet, using the paper as a protective glove. Bingo, amongst the array of medicine bottles and boxes, pills, and toiletries, I spotted a dark brown skinny bottle with no label. I knew it must have been what I was looking for. I quickly grabbed it, pulled out the plastic cork and sniffed the opening. An unpleasant stench hit my nose. Yes, this had to be Lutz's medicine. I put it in my jacket pocket and exited.

Back in my motel I entered my room and called Bruce, hiring him for a new job. I gave him Petra's phone number, told him it was disconnected, asking for new number information, and the location where the phone was used prior to being disconnected. I called the taxi service and checked out from the motel. The taxi took me to the saloon where my rented BMW was still parked. I drove off, hoping nobody would connect me with Keith and Tilly, and their deaths would be quickly concluded as drug overdoses which had become so common lately.

I drove north toward the Oklahoma-Kansas border. Charlie reminded me that the town of Hopkins was mentioned, and this was where I was heading.

I hadn't even reached the Kansas border when my phone rang. It was Bruce. He couldn't obtain any new information regarding the phone number I'd given him.

"The last activity on that phone was from about a month ago, from Hopkins, Kansas. This is strange, Spinner. I can usually track down all calls up to the time when the number is disconnected. It seems like this phone number wasn't used lately at all and was never replaced with another one."

20

BARBARA and MARIA

Driving to Hopkins was uneventful and boring. As I came closer to town the landscape had become increasingly desolate, flat and hypnotically incessant, with fields of native, mostly dried out grasses. It tired me out and I was glad to finally reach the town. At first, I saw nothing unusual. The community seemed to be small, quite rural, with almost no traffic and without anyone walking the streets. The heart of the town was its Main Street, where the majority of activities took place. The town library, local McDonald's restaurant and the motel where I was heading, all had a Main Street addresses. By the time I arrived at Hopkins Motel, the emptiness of my surroundings became even more evident, making me feel like the whole place was forsaken, as if I were visiting a ghost town. Only a few cars parked in front of the buildings testified that the place was alive and kicking, even if not entirely well. I was hungry, but skipped McDonald's, because I first wanted to put down my anchor, which provided me a sense of security, although at times a false one.

No surprise – the front desk was abandoned. I tapped on the reception desk bell and from the back office a skinny person showed up with a friendly nod.

"Welcome to Hopkins," the young woman greeted me. She was dressed in a pink uniform and had fiery red hair with a face full of cute freckles – typical for a person of her complexion.

"Thank you," I said. "I have no reservation, but I hope you might have a room available."

"You bet," she said. "I don't recall if we were ever full."

"You've worked here a long time?"

"Seems like forever. It's our family business," she smiled and nodded. "We were born here, even my parents were never let go."

"What's the population of Hopkins?"

"I suppose a few thousand, give or take a few."

OK, I hoped that was a joke.

"Our rate is $39.95 per night, with a 10% discount for a four-night stay, and we also have weekly and monthly rates."

"I'm not sure how long I'll stay. Let me pay for four nights, and we'll take it from there. As long as there are no spiders in my room, I'll be OK."

"Spiders, you said? Oh no, mister, we have no spiders," she said in a confident voice.

"Good," I smiled. "I am allergic to spiders."

"Then you came to the right place. We have no spiders, or other bugs. No dogs, no cats and no birds."

"Let me guess: you guys don't like animals, right?" I said.

"Oh, it's not our place only, I am talking about the whole town," she explained.

"There must be a very unhappy local veterinarian somewhere down the road," I joked.

"No, such service is not needed," she said seriously.

"What do you mean, what if your dog or cat becomes sick?

"I told you, we have no dogs or cats. Nobody around here does."

"Are you telling me that the entire town is without any pets?"

"That's right, we don't believe in pets."

I didn't want to argue but this declaration puzzled me. She didn't look like she was joking, and yet her statement was impossible to believe. Having pets was not a matter of belief. I decided not to press the issue.

What about horses, I only asked. Nobody had a horse. Chickens? Nope. What about wild animals, birds, bats, coyotes, rabbits, squirrels, what have you?

"I don't think so," she said.

"Spinner, she's right," Charlie kicked in. "You paid no attention, but there were no dogs or birds at all that could be seen since we entered the town limits."

What? What kind of crazy prank was that? By no means was I a biology major, but I knew that without birds and bugs there could be no pollenating taking place, and the entire biosystem would be thrown off balance. In another words, such a ludicrous scenario was not possible. On the motel reception desk was a vase full of flowers and I was just about to point them out to the woman and challenge her to explain to me how this was possible, when I realized that the flowers were artificial. Never mind, bad example.

It was time to stop the chitchat and I asked where the location of recently opened facility was – where the research on zoonotic diseases was conducted.

No, she wouldn't know anything about it. She said it was none of her business. But there was a barber shop down the street and the owner, Eddie, knew everything that went on in town, she said. She further speculated that perhaps I was asking about the military facility which was located out of town. They had nothing to do with the zoo… whatchamacallit diseases.

What about the outbreak of illness there, that was reported on TV? She was vehement that there was no illness outbreak there. What was I talking about? She seemed to be honest and looked at me as if I was turning into a weirdo. I concluded that there must have been a wide and successful cover up. This meant that the situation was either under complete control, or it was getting so bad that the authorities spared no expense to hush things up and prevent a panic.

One way or another, this was disturbing.

"Fine," I said. "Where is this military facility?"

"Fort Montaus?" she asked. "You just take Main Street some five miles down the road. When you get to the intersection at 120th Ave, Main Street changes its name. There will be signs telling you that only military vehicles are allowed."

I thanked her, completed my check-in formalities and went to my room.

I inspected it thoroughly. It was surprisingly clean and bugless. I turned on the TV hoping to hear news about the outbreak and possibly if there was anything on Tilly's and Keith's deaths. I couldn't find any local TV channels, only entertainment and national channels. I found the news. No mentioning of the illness outbreak, nor about the overdose deaths of Tilly and Keith. Odd.

I turned the TV off and from the nightstand drawer pulled out a phone book and the Bible. In the yellow pages, under 'Veterinarians and veterinary hospitals' there were few listings but neither one had the Hopkins address. This confirmed part of the freckled girl's statement. I also flipped through the Bible pages and found several lines and even entire paragraphs at certain places blacked out. The Bible copy resembled a declassified document which was released to the public, but still partially censored. This was crazy.

Charlie was not shy in expressing his views on all this, and his thoughts went along with mine, so I did not engage in much conversation.

I took a quick shower and decided to skip the meal and check out Fort Montaus.

Down in the lobby another small surprise. It had been less than an hour since I spoke to the freckled girl, and she was still tending reception but wearing completely different color clothing. I usually notice details like these. What the hell? I remembered that she was in pink when I first saw her, and now she was in yellow and red clothes. This added to my conviction that the place was crazy. It bothered me, and I asked: "Pardon me, didn't you just change your clothes?"

She smiled. "No, I didn't."

Now she had even lied to me, this was getting worse and more irritating by the minute.

"I could swear when we talked while ago, that you had a pink shirt on, and now you are in a red and yellow sweater," I said.

She kept smiling. "Amazing, isn't it? I can explain. You see, you and I never met, you talked to my twin sister Barbara. I just took over. I am Maria."

Wow. This came as a relief. They sure were look-alikes. Sometimes things appeared puzzling at first but could be explained in an amazingly simple way.

"My sister said you were interested in Fort Montaus?" she asked.

"Yes, I'm thinking to check the place out. I'd like to meet with somebody there."

"I hope you have an invitation. They are pretty discrete and secretive. They don't even come to town much. If you keep driving on the restricted road uninvited, you could be arrested. It happened to some curious local people before."

"No invitation. If that's the only way to get in touch, I might do just that."

"Your call. Good luck!" she said and smiled again.

Driving down Main Street I looked around to see any animal presence. No luck. I thought it was impossible not to see any birds. There were some trees along the road, and one would expect to see at least few birds around, but nothing.

"Spinner, I think she is correct – this place is clear of animals," Charlie commented.

"But this is nonsense," I argued. "This can't be."

I kept driving down Main Street and soon I was out of town. My GPS was showing that Main Street ended at 120th Ave, at a 'T' intersection. The landscape was flat and dull, but in front of me in the distance, I saw a hill. There were no buildings on either side of the road; I was out in the country. Gradually the terrain became mountainous and more wooded. The road was straight but bumpy. It also narrowed when I got to the intersection at 120th Ave. Contrary to GPS the road continued straight ahead. Across I saw four prominent signs posted on the right side, large enough to be easily readable from where I was. The biggest one read:

WARNING – Restricted Area
and the other one,
U.S. MILITARY FACILITY
Smaller signs carried messages:
ENTERING FORT MONTAUS AREA
And:
MILITARY VEHICLES ONLY BEYOND THIS POINT

There was no traffic.

"Do you really want to do it?" Charlie voiced the question.

"What else can I do?" I responded. "I don't know any other way to get in touch with them, and after all I've been through, I can't just roll over and play dead."

Charlie said nothing, and I asked him: "Do you agree? Do you have a better idea?"

He hesitated for a moment and said: "Not really. I told you this didn't look like a good idea to me in a first place, but I suppose since you came this far, it would be foolish not to proceed."

"All right, Charlie! Here we go."

And I drove across the intersection and entered the restricted part of the road. Nothing was different than the previously traveled section. No additional road signage, not even a speed limit posted, no parking zone information. After a half a mile or so the road further narrowed down to a single lane. It made me wonder what they did when two cars traveling in opposite directions met. Both sides of the road were framed with a ditch and it looked like it would be a problem for two vehicles to pass each other.

I continued driving on the prohibited area and the landscape became more densely wooded. I wouldn't call it a forest but there were more and more maple trees around me. The road slightly curved to the left. I saw it was blocked by chain link fencing stretched across it. I stopped my car and exited. The chain link fence extended to both sides and disappeared behind the trees. The road behind the fence looked just the same as on my side of it. The fence in front of me was actually a gate, and the whole barrier was about eleven feet of chain link fencing with a razor wire roll on the top. There were no other structures in sight, not even a cabin with security guards. To my surprise I couldn't see any cameras around, although I knew there must be some warning system in place. On the gate was more signage, and I read them all.

PHOTOGRAPHING OF THIS AREA STRICTLY PROHIBITED
NO OPEN TOE SHOES BEYOND THIS POINT

THIS FACILITY CONTAINS ONE OR MORE CHEMICALS
KNOWN TO THE STATE OF KANSAS TO CAUSE
CANCER BIRTH DEFECTS OR REPRODUCTIVE HARM

BIOHAZARD WARNING
MILITARY CONTROLLED ZONE BEYOND THIS POINT
FALLOUT SHELTER

I was just about to finish reading all this signage on the gate, when out of nowhere I heard a voice coming from very close behind me: "May I help you?"

21

SCOTT and ROBERTO

I turned around and came face to face with a young man in a military uniform. He was watching me carefully, probably evaluating whether I posed any threat. He was so young that he couldn't be very experienced. However, he was dead serious and determined. "What are you doing here?" he asked in a firm voice. I probably shouldn't have answered the way I did, but something made me say: "I come in peace."

His eyes opened wider. Obviously, he was familiar with this phrase from classic science fiction. I continued: "Take me to your leader."

It was only me who found this funny. The young soldier put up an angry face, obviously thinking I was making fun of him. Charlie spoke: "Spinner, this is not the best time for cracking stupid jokes."

The soldier put his hand on the gun and commanded me: "Sir, you need to surrender your car keys. Now."

I waved toward the car. "In the car, in the ignition," I said. While keeping an eye on me, he peeked through the driver's side window and verified I told the truth. I realized the young man was taking his duty seriously and decided not to joke any more.

"Sorry, I didn't mean to offend you. What is your name, son? What do you want me to do?"

"I'm not your son. Just don't move and wait here," he said. We spent the next minute or so in silence. He kept measuring me up with his eyes.

I heard a vehicle approaching from the other side of the fence. A military jeep showed up with two uniformed people in it. The driver remained in the vehicle, and the other man jumped out. He was in full military gear. The motorized gate began sliding to the side, and soon there was no barrier between us.

The young soldier saluted and pointed to the BMW. "Sir, the keys are in the ignition."

"Good. Take it to yard east number two," he nodded to the young soldier, and then showed me the way to the jeep. "And you, get in."

He pointed to the back seat of the jeep. I sat there and he blindfolded me. A wave of panic came over me, but Charlie's words relaxed me a bit. "This isn't as bad as it seems, Spinner. They don't want you to see their facility, which means they won't kill you and you will be let go, eventually."

After what seemed a long and bumpy ride, the vehicle stopped. My blindfold prevented me seeing anything, but I heard the sound of a metal door moving. The jeep started and stopped again. They led me out of it and walked me into a building. We passed through a few doors. Finally, they helped me sit down. My blindfold was removed.

"Don't move. Wait here," said the soldier who came out of the jeep. He left the room. I wasn't restrained with handcuffs, nor was I tied to a chair. They must have figured out I was no threat.

I looked around. I was sitting at the metal table facing the wall with a mirror through which I could be observed from the other side. This was, no doubt, the interrogation room. The escape door was to my right. I had no plans to escape. I came to get in touch with someone in charge and complete my mission by giving Petra the remedy and letting them have the rest for mass production as needed. They didn't have to give me a medal, but some kind of recognition, even in the form of simple 'thank you' would do. Maybe Petra would consider breaking up with Mr. Laos and getting back with me… Ha-ha! Keep dreaming, Spinner, and hope that the girl would dump a billionaire and come back to me.

The door opened and a new person in military dress stepped in. I had no idea about different military ranks, but this one had some important looking insignia on his sleeve. He was a strong, tall person in his early thirties, and looked self-confident. Yes, he was someone in charge. He sat in a chair across the table. The room was lit by the high neon light and not pointed directly in my face. I felt like a person who was involved in a conversation rather than a suspect about to be questioned.

The man was studying me silently and without any introduction started questioning me. "Why did you drive through the restricted zone?"

Charlie immediately took the role of my attorney and said: "Answer only what he asks you. Don't try to take control of the conversation. Remember, what he asks, you answer. No more, no less. Don't rush with your answers."

I'll try, Charlie. But my goal was to skip the insignificant details and get down to business as soon as possible. After all, I came here voluntarily, and this was the only way I could get in touch with them.

"I am here to end the wrath of the mandrill," I said, right away regretting what I said. He would not know what I was talking about and would only think that I was crazy.

He was looking at me as if trying to figure out if I was serious or not. His face revealed nothing. "What is that?"

"That is Mr. Laos' description of what has happened," I said, hoping the Laos' name would ring a bell.

"Who is Mr. Laos?"

"He is the guy who donated this land to the government. About one thousand acres. This property was owned by him."

The man didn't move a muscle. "When did he do that?"

"I'd say two-three months ago. I'm not sure. Sometime before they closed Duke of Prunes down and moved here."

"This fort has been here from the Sixties; it was established about 70 years ago," the interviewer finally shared some information.

This was confusing, but Charlie came to the rescue. "Spinner, keep in mind there could be a simple explanation for this. Maybe Mr. Laos' property is located nearby this fort, who knows. Maybe this guy knows nothing about it."

Maybe. But I was also losing my patience. "C'mon, you guys don't have to keep your coverup from me. I was present when the first outbreak happened, at the Chicago Zoo, when Lutz threw his germs at us and Lydia set him on fire. Ask Mr. Laos to confirm this."

"Too much information, Spinner. He didn't ask you this," Charlie said.

I knew that, but I wanted to speed up their damn investigation and have them realize that I know much about what was going on, and to let me help them with a cure. I wanted to see Petra again.

The man was looking at me with his sharp eyes, and I couldn't figure out what effect, if any, my words had on him. He paused again, and finally asked: "What is your name?"

"Spinner Walker. And yours?"

"I am Major Scott Clandon."

I assumed people on the other side of the mirror were punching my name in their computers and getting information about me. That would speed up the hoopla, and they should soon realize that I was not a total outsider. Then the Major spoke again: "Empty your pockets and put everything you have with you here on this table."

Really? I stood up and took out the contents of my pockets: wallet, some change, the keys from my Ceilings apartment, motel key, Lutz's bottle with medicine, and the necklace.

The man visually inspected my possessions but made no attempt to pick them up.

I pointed toward the bottle. "This is the remedy for the current outbreak. Lutz gave it to his girlfriend, and I got it from her. I came to give it to Petra, my ex-girlfriend who works here – she is infected, but I hope still alive and in the hospital. We need to treat her with this, and you can use the rest and go into production and cure the other infected people, or should I say women."

"In what department does your ex-girlfriend work?"

"I can't recall precisely the name…" I started but Charlie interrupted. "I know it, Spinner. It's called Federal Animal Disorder Research Center."

"Oh yes, wait a minute," I quickly said. "I think it's called Federal Animal Disorder Research Center. Lutz never arrived there – he managed to ship himself to his brother who works at the Chicago Zoo."

Major Clandon seemed to be unimpressed with my statement, or at least I saw no change in his behavior.

"Tell me more about Lutz."

"He was a fanimal who died at the Chicago Zoo where he released the germs he created, and caused the illness outbreak there, and now here."

"Fanimal?"

"Jesus, I thought you would know all about this. I need to talk to someone who has access to classified data. Yes, fanimal. Two species fused together. Lutz was fused with a mandrill. That's why Mr. Laos called this outbreak the wrath of the mandrill."

"How did you get involved in all this?"

"That is a long story. Listen, we are wasting time here, and it might be too late for Petra, and the other infected women."

"And there were two outbreaks of the disease, you said?"

"One was in Chicago, and another one was here. It was all over TV, before you people hushed up the story. Please ask about this Mr.

132

Laos. His daughter is also infected, and he took her to Hong Kong. I think they might still be there."

"And this bottle contains the remedy for the disease?"

"Yes. I got it because before his death Lutz said that he gave it to Tilly, his girlfriend, and I found her and got the bottle from her."

"Where is she now?"

"In Oklahoma. That isn't important now. I came to Hopkins after I heard on TV about the second outbreak. I called Petra and she told me that she was also infected and in a local hospital, but I have no idea where that is. You later confiscated and disconnected her cellphone number."

"Where did you stay in Hopkins?"

"In the motel on Main Street. Barbara and Maria told me about this base. I spoke to both of them."

For the first time I saw a change in the man's behavior, coming in the form of his eyebrows, which jumped some inch or so up on his forehead.

"You talked to Maria?"

I nodded. "Yes, they are twins, right? Nice girls."

The man shook his head a bit. "They were twins all right, but Maria was run over by a car and killed when she was a six-year-old, some dozen or more years ago."

I began feeling some strange tingling on my skin, very uncomfortable. What the hell? This was unreal.

"C'mon Spinner, don't lose your marbles now," Charlie said. "For some reason Barbara told you she was her twin. I bet she is missing her sister a lot and sometime takes her role in front of people who don't know what happened."

Charlie's words put me at ease again. He was right: Things have explanations even if they look strange or impossible at first look.

Major Clandon got up. "I'll take this bottle, and you wait here," he said.

He reached for the bottle and pointed to the necklace. "What is this?"

I jumped from my chair and shouted: "Don't touch it!"

It was too late. He already had the necklace in his hand. Surprised by my panicky shriek, he dropped the necklace back on the table. At that moment, from the side wall something like a bolt of lightning was instantly fired, blinding me and hitting on the side of my body, causing me excruciating pain. I was down on the ground, almost knocked cold.

Shit! It was some kind of mechanism designed to protect the investigator from the unruly person who was being interrogated. The pain went away quickly – it was some kind of electric shock that incapacitated me, if only for a short time. I got up from the ground and sat back in my chair.

The Major regained his posture, and was sitting again across from me, frozen face without showing any emotion.

"Major, you're dead man!" I announced.

"Are you threatening me?" he asked angrily.

Shit! If I had to explain the necklace, this would make the whole story more complicated and add to the confusion. I was frustrated and couldn't figure out if he really knew nothing about what I was telling him, or was he continuing to cover up the outbreak of the illness because I couldn't convince him about my involvement.

"Nothing," I said. "You shouldn't have touched the necklace."

"You touched it too. I will take the bottle now," he said.

I said nothing and he took the bottle, got up and went to the door. The door opened and he exited. Another person showed up. This one was in civilian clothes, long hair, glasses and an unshaven face. His hippie look was sharply different from the well-groomed and highly disciplined U.S. military. I wondered, what was the connection?

He approached my table and said: "My name is Dr. Roberto Montenegro. You and I need to have a serious talk about your delusions."

22

FUTURE and NOW

"Careful, Spinner," Charlie warned. "This guy could put you in the nuthouse for good."

A wave of anger came over me. These idiots seemed to be ready to sacrifice my own wellbeing in order to keep a lid on the outbreak. What the hell was going on? I knew I had to control myself, and not give them a real reason for putting me away.

"And why am I delusional?" I asked, looking at this hippie doctor in the eyes. I disliked this person, who was probably a self-proclaimed genius who managed to convince others of his brilliance and earned the privilege to walk around in casual clothes making statements like 'look at me, I am so special I can do whatever I want.' No, I didn't like this man.

"I'm not sure yet," he answered. "This is what I need to figure out. Don't look so upset, just answer my questions."

"What do you want to know?"

"Is there anything else unusual, you encountered at Hopkins motel?"

"You mean other than talking to Maria, who you people told me died years ago?"

"Yes."

"You know, there could be another explanation for that, rather than declaring me delusional. It could be her twin is longing for her sister and at times pretending to be her, and that way keeping the memory of her alive?"

"You're right, that might be it."

"To answer your question, there were also other oddities as well," I continued.

"Such as?"

"The Bible. In my room there was a Bible with censored parts. At places the entire paragraphs were blacked out. I found this unusual, and you might call it delusional."

"This can be easily verified. Do you have any theories why somebody would censor the Bible?'

"Certainly. For example, my mother is very religious, fanatically religious. I saw her doing unusual things, so I can imagine that a person with similar beliefs could want to black out the segments of the Bible they disagree with. My mother would even criticize the Pope for being too progressive."

"Bravo, Spinner," Charlie praised me.

"Interesting," said Dr. Montenegro. "Anything else?"

"Yes," I said. "The absence of animals in Hopkins. Nobody has dogs or cats, there was no birds flying around, not even bugs. I think you and your damned experiments caused that. They were eradicated. You should acknowledge this and accept that I came here to help you with the medicine that would cure infected people. Instead, you are stubbornly continuing your coverup and calling me delusional."

Dr. Montenegro nodded, seemingly approving my words. "Mr. Walker," he said. "What would you say if I took you right now back to Hopkins, and showed you that there are people with pets there, and birds flying around like everywhere else?"

"You do that, and I would acknowledge that I am delusional. But I don't think you can do that."

"Actually, I can. I assure you – there are cats, bugs, birds, horses, and more there in town right now. But frankly, this isn't the reason why I thought you may be delusional."

"What is it, then?" I asked.

"It was what you said to Major Clandon a few minutes ago. I observed your interview with him from the other side of this mirror. You said that the Duke of Prunes was closed down, and Mr. Laos was in Hong Kong with his sick daughter, and so forth. What would you say if I told you that two days ago, I returned from my visit to Duke of Prunes? That place is not closed down, and Mr. Laos was there and not in Hong Kong. I was at the dinner attended also by his daughter and she was not ill? Just about everything else you told Major Clandon in this regard simply didn't happen."

It became clear to me this man was delusional, not me. I couldn't figure out why they were so determined to negate what really happened, and why. "I think you are a liar because this can't be. What I told the Major was the truth."

"And you see, everything I said about my visit to Duke of Prunes is also the truth. This is why I thought you might me delusional. You obviously think we are covering up some outbreak of illness while we are not. You can't cover up something that didn't happen."

I was swept off my feet. I realized that no matter what, they were not going to change their story, and I was going to lose. I was going to be declared delusional and thrown into an asylum. Charlie was right – I should have minded my own business and to hell with helping others. It became clear that something big must have been behind all this, when they were so adamant about continuing their scheme. I tried one more time to convince him I was telling the truth.

"I see where this is going," I said angrily. "For whatever reason, you want to keep me out of it. To you, I am crazy, case closed. But I can prove to you that it's you who isn't telling the truth. If you think you are, then you are insane, and not me. I gave Mr. Laos the address where Lutz mailed the crate with the fanimal mandrill in it, and he paid me a lot of money for that. A million dollars. This morning I looked at my bank account online, and this money is there. You can easily verify how I got it. You also have the medication Lutz made and if you analyze it, I bet it would have some original properties that are not available anywhere else. This proves that I'm telling the truth, and you aren't. Now, I will no longer answer any more questions without my lawyer present. I don't have one yet, but I'll hire the best one my money can get. And I regret I was trying to help because you people don't deserve it and should go to hell."

The hippie doctor let me finish my outburst without interrupting. He even had an agreeable expression on his face. Maybe I had begun to convince him that I was honest? Perhaps, but I wouldn't bet on it.

"Mr. Walker, I came to talk to you because I wasn't a 100% convinced you were delusional. I really returned from Duke of Prunes two days ago, so everything you said sounded like the story of a demented individual. However, something that both you and Mr. Laos said, prevented me from undoubtedly pronouncing you insane. He was concerned about two pieces of the shipment that didn't reach their designated destination. One was this crate with the mandrill, just as you indicated, and Mr. Laos was very worried not knowing where this shipment went. This goes along the lines of what you said to Major Clandon. You see, I went there because Duke of Prunes is indeed in the process of closing down and moving here, to the property adjacent to this base. But this hasn't happened yet. Nothing that you described happened. You seem to be talking about matter that might occur in the future and not about stuff already materialized."

Oh my God. I realized how inconceivable it was what he was talking about. "But this is not possible. Is it?" I asked.

"I don't know. Was it possible you witnessed events that will happen sometime in the near future? Having an open scientific mind, I could speculate that you somehow, spontaneously acquired the ability to participate in the events within different time frames. You are apparently unaware of this. Even more, if you really spoke to Maria who would be about twenty now, for a short while you became a part of a different reality in which she didn't die in a car accident. I don't know what it is, but you will have to stay here and let us try to figure it out. I hope you realize how important this is. We want answers to what is happening to you, what triggered your departures from 'now' and what made it possible for you to return, as well as what caused it in a first place. But, before anything else, we have to take advantage of what we already know. We need to prevent people being infected with the unknown viruses and becoming sick. If your story is true, and I now lean toward 'yes,' we have a unique opportunity to avoid bad things from happening. We know that Lutz is in the Chicago Zoo, and we should be able to stop him from releasing the germs so nothing of what you've experienced would take place. Your girlfriend would never become sick and quarantined in the hospital, and nobody would die."

I was stunned. I couldn't comprehend all the consequences if what this guy said was true. But Charlie had a quick idea. "Spinner, this means Petra wouldn't become Mr. Laos' girlfriend either," he said.

This was good.

"But if nothing you experienced will happen, then the money Mr. Laos paid you will also be gone," Charlie continued.

True. This was bad.

"And they want to keep you here, Spinner, as a guinea pig. They want to experiment on you. Probably indefinitely. You will be a prisoner of science for life," Charlie mercilessly completed his assessment.

Wow. This was ugly. I sure didn't like what Dr. Montenegro said about keeping me there to be a subject of their endless research. No doubt, this would happen. I realized how important I had become. I was unique. Was I really visiting the future? If so, I didn't notice any changes in reality. How did this happen? And why me? Had I been exposed to something that was causing this? Was this a blessing or a curse? Would it happen again? Questions without answers.

My thoughts were interrupted by blinking lights, and the sound of a siren.

"Away from the table!" Charlie said and I knew what he meant. I pushed my chair away and narrowly avoided the bolt of lightning and shock that was again automatically fired from the wall. I jumped from the chair and grabbed my possessions from the table.

"What are you doing?" Dr. Montenegro asked. He also jumped from his chair and tried to prevent me in my quest to reach the door. I pushed him aside and he fell on the floor. The door opened and a person shouted just before I hit him: "Major Clandon electrocuted himself! What…"

The necklace! That was my necklace at work, and I was so glad that I took it from the table and had it in my pocket. I hit the man in the doorway and pushed him aside, and thanks to the surprise factor managed to pass him. I was in the corridor not really knowing what my escape route would be. Charlie, as always, came to the rescue. "To your left. There is a door with an 'Exit' sign."

I rushed toward that door, opened it and found myself outside, in a large yard. Among several parked vehicles I saw my BMW and I ran to it begging that the keys were still in the ignition.

They were, and I quickly started the engine, pressing the pedal to the metal. I was determined to escape this place – I would not become a prisoner for something I was not guilty of.

Charlie helped me get to the road that lead back to Main Street and I was driving fast. Luckily there was nobody else on that road and soon I saw the familiar fence/gate blocking the road. I hoped my car was strong enough to kick the gate open without seriously damaging the machine. I supposed I was right, but I never had a chance to test it. As I came close to the gate and increased my speed, a few feet before hitting the gate a metal barrier triggered by some automatic detecting system popped up from the road and the car hit it and came to a violent stop. An airbag was deployed preventing me from hitting my head on the steering wheel and the dashboard. But from the force of the impact I did momentarily passed out.

When I opened my eyes everything around me was pitch dark – I couldn't see anything. Was I blind? Or was I imprisoned in the dark room? I couldn't tell. Was I even alive? Why did I feel no pain? Where was I? When was I? Who was I? And why me?

PART 3: HAPPY ENDING

23

FATHER and SON

I am sitting at a library desk, flipping through the national daily newspapers, looking for articles everybody else can freely find and read, and yet, what I am doing is spying. To me this is a meaningless and dull job and I'm doing it only as a favor to my father. Certainly, this doesn't sound like a dangerous activity, but I know I could be prosecuted for what I am doing.

It is surprising how many American free-press articles frequently contain information foreign governments would deem classified and as such would have been carefully guarded in their own countries. Because of the sheer quantity of material to be scrutinized, many low-level extras, such as myself, are employed to initially comb through the vast material available, pouring daily out of our newsrooms.

It is prohibited to discuss details on topics I am searching through and looking for, and what guidelines I follow in this process. Let's just say that after identifying potential articles of interest all I do is record newspaper titles, dates, page numbers where they appear, and article headlines. I am good at this and I regularly discover articles fitting the areas of interest.

I am getting tense because I expect my dad to meet me here. He is a bit late, and this increases my nervousness. We normally don't communicate much, and this contributes to my feeling slightly apprehensive. I guess he has something important to tell me.

Finally, here he is, waking toward me, trying to look away from the security camera. The picture looks awkward. He is missing his left arm, which he never replaced with an artificial device, as if wanting to draw attention to his disability. I never saw him attempting to camouflage his disadvantage. To the contrary – he often wears short sleeve shirts, letting his stump protrude, which naturally draws everybody's attention. This is odd, taking into consideration that he is involved in activities where keeping a low profile is the norm.

"Hi son," he says and sits across the round table I occupy.

"Hi," I nod, looking around. It seems that the few library patrons in the room are focused on their own business and his entry drew no attention.

"Found anything interesting?" he asks, looking at my notebook from his side of the table.

"Only a few so far."

"Good. Good!" he says.

He looks around to see if people are far enough not to hear our conversation. He even leans over the table toward me so he can speak quietly. I also lean toward him and we are looking at each other from a close distance. I can smell him. I notice the signs of his aging. He has wrinkles on his forehead and neck. I see grey hair on his head, and that he didn't shave for a day or two. I look at his eyes. They look tired and sad. He is ready to share something confidential.

"What is it?" I say, smelling rats.

He quietly outlines an additional task for me. I look at him in disbelief. Is he joking, is he crazy, or what? No, he is dead serious. He is asking me to get rid of an individual who is posing a great danger to the country. I am not sure what country he is talking about – America or Latvia, where he has lived for a long time, and where I was born. I suspect he is a double agent. He is using the word 'removing,' not 'murdering,' 'killing,' or 'assassinating.'

I shake my head. "I am not into this, Dad. You will have to find someone else, or do it yourself," I say.

He can't do it because of his handicap and when that person is whacked, he will be a main suspect. He has to secure a solid alibi for the time when this takes place. The person in question has scheduled a meeting during which will present the list of people's names and they will be subsequently arrested and prosecuted. Some of them will face the death penalty. One name on that list is my father's.

"I need your help, and you can do it, son," he says. "I have a detailed plan of how, when and where."

"Tell him to get lost, Spinner," says Charlie, my alter ego.

Yeah, but this is my father. And I know I owe him, although I can't remember for what.

"I can't, I can't do it, I really can't," I tell him.

"Yes, you can," father replies. "This person is no good and if arrested would anyway be sentenced to life in prison."

"What kind of father would push his son into becoming a murderer, Spinner?" Charlie is persistent. "You owe him nothing, he didn't want to marry your mother, he didn't care for you whatsoever, and now he wants to use you. He is your father, but he is no good. Tell him to get lost."

I say nothing, and my father pulls an envelope from his pants back pocket: "Read this. It's cryptic but you will understand what it says. This will be easy for you to do."

"Why would this be easy for me to do?"

"Because the target is a woman, Spinner. And you already know how much trouble women are. She is an older person, nobody you know, and nobody you would fall in love with. You can make it look like an accident. You have that necklace. It'll be easy to make it look like an accident, Spinner. You can use that necklace to get the job done."

And without waiting for my reply he gets up from his chair and walks away, toward the library exit door, so I had no chance to ask him how the hell he knows about the necklace. Who the hell told him about that damn necklace?

24

LIONS and ELEPHANTS

In the middle of their enclosure the impressive looking pair of lions are busy mating. We are watching from the viewing deck along with a large crowd of visitors. Some people are laughing, some seem slightly embarrassed. Adult family members accompanied by small children asking questions are showing signs of discomfort. They carefully select words, trying to satisfy their kids curiosity and explain what is taking place.

The mating ritual of majestic cats ends abruptly, as the lioness has had enough. She angrily shakes her body and jumps aside to get the large male off of her back. His impressive black mane also shakes, and his long white canines, visible from his open mouth, shine. He lets out a deep, triumphant roar. He also seems displeased that the action is over.

It is a beautiful spring day, not too warm, and many zoo animals are in a romantic mood. Although confined within a limited space they are comfortable enough to search for a mate and secure continuance of their kind.

We get to the elephant habitat and see a large African bull nervously walking around. His enormous penis is extended almost to the ground, as he begins to urinate. I hear one child telling his father 'wow, Dad, look at this elephant! I think he is a boy, yes, he's definitively a boy!'

I can't help but giggle and everybody else who heard the little boy's remark is laughing too. Petra put her arm on mine and laughingly comments: "He sure is!"

We walk toward the monkey habitat and find an especially large crowd in front of their outdoor enclosures. Everybody wants to watch the playful monkeys. They never run out of new ideas to entertain themselves and the audience. Their outdoor area habitats are connected to an old building where the monkeys are kept during the night and in cold weather. The building is open to the public, and we pass through it stopping at different cages built on both sides of the corridor. All the cages are heavily secured with double chain-link fence, and a concrete floor extends into them. Not even the wooden logs, straw, ropes and other furnishings can disguise the old-fashioned appearance of these enclosures. The monkeys have access to both the outside and inside part of their habitat and I am surprised that many specimens choose to remain inside. I would think that outdoors living would be their preferential choice. There are macaques, baboons, colobus monkeys and more.

We approach one smaller cage and in it quietly sitting on a porch is a single monkey, a mandrill. With a colorful face and smart eyes, he looks sad and doesn't move. Some visitors are trying to get him to react by waving, screaming and gesturing but he remains motionless. Thinking. Suddenly, he charges the fence. His eyes are full of wrath. He then calms down and turns away, paying no attention to us. An uncomfortable feeling overwhelms me. He looks so intelligent. I know he is the largest monkey species; the big apes are the only ones larger than mandrills. Turning his head toward us a little bit, he observes the noisy audience with eyes reflecting contempt and boredom. Finally, he turns his head back, facing the wall.

We quickly take off and I realize Petra is having no pleasure in seeing an animal of such magnificent appearance and posture solitary displayed in small quarters.

We drive home and discuss our zoo visit.

"Seeing that poor mandrill is frightening and is just killing me," she says, and I agree. I am becoming more sympathetic to her critical views about wild animals in captivity.

We are at home and I'd like to take a shower, because I'm all sweaty. I take my clothes off. She looks at me and says, "A boy, you definitively look like a boy to me."

We laugh, and I take a quick shower anticipating our intimate encounter after a long dry spell.

I exit the bathroom, wearing the towel around my waist. I see Petra messing around my clothes. She's emptied my pockets.

"What are you doing?" I ask.

"Getting ready to do the laundry."

I become upset. It's not so much that she picks such a peculiar time to do the laundry, but the fact that in her hand she holds my Indian necklace. This is not good. Not good at all.

"Laundry? Now?" I ask.

"This necklace," she says. "Where did you get it? Is it for me?"

I am angry. You touched it. Yes, now it has to be for you. I nervously hope she comes out of this alive. I know what she thinks. The necklace isn't particularly attractive, not even to me. She thinks she has to put on an act and pretend that she likes it. But all this is not important. She doesn't know there is more to it than meets the eye.

"Yes, it's for you," I say. "But you shouldn't have touched it. I have to make you now a designated keeper of the necklace."

"Thank you," she says theatrically, with a tone of voice clearly showing that she is uncertain why am I telling a joke with such a serious face.

Darling, this is no joke. I would have more explaining to do. I hope she will believe me that she should never let anyone else touch or wear this necklace. But this can wait. I want to see that she survives. She was in contact with the necklace before I formally promoted her to be the designated keeper of it, and I am not sure if my proclamation will work retroactively. I don't know if her life is in jeopardy or not. However, there is nothing I can do.

I sit on the sofa, wearing nothing but a towel, observing Petra and waiting to see if anything happens.

25

MAHOGANY and JUDGE

It is my first time in an Illinois courtroom as a defendant. It's my first time in any courtroom, period. Mahogany everywhere. Neither the prosecution nor the defense brought any witnesses. This is a public hearing, but only a few people are in the audience. My lawyer is next to me; however I feel like I am alone. I am accused of vandalism that led to death. They wrapped up their story in legal terms, essentially meaning the same bullshit. This is, of course, ridiculous. The world seems to have gone mad. They just slap unsubstantiated charges on me, simply because they were too lazy to properly dig into the subject matter.

I am pissed off and in a bad mood. My attorney reminds me to behave and that being arrogant is not helping my case. Charlie is supportive and angry at what is happening. He is speaking in a female tone of voice, which is how he expresses his annoyance. I have my back turned to the audience. I don't know these people or for what perverse reason they want to waste their time here, but I also recognized Petra in the small crowd when I entered the courtroom.

She is sitting in the first row behind me, wearing some strangely shaped female hat I never saw before. Her looks resemble that of a certain English royal family member.

The hearing begins with 'all rise' phrase, and I am listening to a lengthy introductory procedure, hoping they will cut the crap and get to the point. But that doesn't happen. Finally comes part where they accuse me of breaking into the Chicago Zoo's monkey house, and setting the building on fire, causing a rare mandrill to die, along with several other monkeys in the building. Lots of blah-blah. Reckless endangerment, breaking and entering, destruction of public property, are some of the words they use, and I understand. They seem to enjoy throwing around a mix of legal and bureaucratic vocabulary, which probably makes them feel important, but in my book, they are bunch of idiots.

My insistence on examining Lydia's dead body, or to get Walter and Mr. Laos as witnesses, was to no avail. There is no evidence Lydia ever existed, and both Mr. Laos and Walter are irrelevant to the case and out of the country anyway.

The whole shebang is an apparent continued coverup, and I am chosen to be a scapegoat, although all I did was try to help.

Instead of recognizing my nobility in trying to save that damned monkey, they attempt to ridicule me for being sloppy because I also almost died in the very fire I allegedly caused. The prosecution asks for five years imprisonment and payment of damages caused by the building fire, restitution for replacement of deceased monkeys, veterinary costs for dealing with other injured monkeys, my own medical bills for smoke inhalation treatment, and court costs.

"If these assholes get what they are asking for, say goodbye to your million," says Charlie in his female voice, depicting irritation.

My attorney is an idiot. He wanted to base our defense on temporary insanity, and I thought this was insane. He is a slit-eyed skinny individual with a face resembling a red fox, and wearing a suit smelling of mothballs. Where and how the hell did I get this guy?

"Don't try to convince them that you were not temporarily insane," Charlie warned.

"Why not?" I asked loudly, causing my attorney to open his eyes a bit wider.

"It's too dangerous a route to take. It might give them an idea. What if they agree with you? They might say 'we agree, your Honor, the defendant is not temporarily insane but permanently.' And off you go, wind up in an asylum for life," Charlie explained.

They also denied Petra as my witness. They said she had nothing to do with this – she wasn't at the zoo when fire started. I know where she was. Memory of that is painful. While I was trying to save that damn fanimal, Lutz, from burning alive, she was in a hotel, in bed with her billionaire lover. Each time I think of that, a tide of anger overcomes me. Only when he dumped her, she came crawling back. We both cried and cried and wound up in bed, which made Charlie even happier than me. He was always a little voyeuristic, and I hoped Petra forgot that we were practically in a ménage à trois relationship.

Charlie thought that she came back to me because I saved her ass when I delivered the remedy for her illness. This, and the fact that Mr. Laos never fell head over heels for her and wouldn't take her with him to Hong Kong, contributed to her reasoning that 'Spinner in her bed is better than a billionaire in Hong Kong.'

I drifted away with my thoughts and paid little attention to what was going on in the courtroom. This all looks insane and I know I have little chance of winning this nightmare. My defense is based on lack of evidence that it was me who caused the fire. The prosecution can't prove that the Molotov cocktail used to ignite the inferno belonged to me. There was also a purse found there, which I know was Lydia's, and the prosecution has a hard time explaining where this badly burnt purse came from. My attorney also points out that I had no prior convictions.

The judge retires to his chamber where he probably pretends to think about this case and comes up with a verdict to serve justice.

This is just a charade to continue the coverup and the fuckup caused by Lutz's release of that damn virus. I'd wish I listened to Charlie when he suggested I shouldn't stick my nose where it didn't belong. Yes, I got Petra back, but what good will this do if I am thrown into jail?

"All rise!" the bailiff announces. "This court is now again in session."

And the judge, bless his heart, proclaims that I am acquitted of all charges. My attorney raises his hands and begins some ridiculous joyful victory dance. He tries to hug me. I can't believe what I just heard. Am I free to go? Not really, the judge continues. I am immediately going to be extradited to Oklahoma where I am wanted as a fugitive suspect in a burglary case which ended in the murder of a couple.

I am surprised there is no usual knot forming in my stomach, like every time when I get myself in trouble, because I know what the judge is talking about – Lutz's dead ex-girlfriend Tilly, and her crazy, dead boyfriend Keith.

26

BEFORE and DISTANCE

I hear voices. I am trying to open my eyes but can't. I feel nothing. I am neither cold nor warm. I don't feel my extremities. I am not hungry, nor thirsty. I am only a thought. I am floating someplace in between, and I can't figure out where this 'between' is. Likely, I am stuck somewhere between life and death. I have almost no memory of what occurred. I try to remember what happened to me, and I see a white airbag in my face. Slow motion. Yes, a car accident. My accident. I know now. I tried to escape the military base. I know everything. Thoughts about this don't excite me. Not only am I physically flat but emotionally as well. But I am reasoning now. And I hear voices, again.

Somebody is talking to me, but I don't understand the words. I think I've heard this voice before. 'Before' is a word I know, but its meaning doesn't apply. I do have a concept of time, but I am not part of it. Time doesn't exist where I am. I am not even in the 'now.' I am trying to connect my perception of past, present and future. I hear voices again, coming from a distance, and I can't understand them. I know the 'distance' is a spatial term. I am slowly recovering my senses. The voices sound closer and clearer, but I am still unable to understand them. I can't tell if they are female or male sounds. I am not tired; I have no feelings about my body and surroundings. I slowly descend back into the black oblivion of nothing.

I open my eyes and see a blurry picture of a darkened place. I recognize the ceiling with light fixture although it remains out of focus. I hear beeping. I am not moving. Because I am looking at the ceiling, I conclude I must be laying on my back. I can't move my head, and I don't feel my arms or legs. I hear voices. I understand them better.

"Jesus, he seems to be coming out of a coma," I hear, recognizing it was a female who said it.

I am not Jesus. My name is Spinner.

"Spinner," someone else says. Yes. I begin to understand what the voice is saying. "We are talking to you all the time. We don't know if you heard or remember any of this. You were in a bad car accident. You are still not out of the woods. More surgeries await you. Your body was pancaked, and you had multiple bone fractures. Some of your internal organs are in a bad shape. Your lung collapsed and damaged your heart. We transplanted these organs into you. It was an urgent procedure. It had to be done right away and now you have an implanted left lung and heart. The donor was Petra. She died shortly before your accident and she was an organ donor. Your head also received a severe concussion. We don't know yet how your cognitive abilities were affected."

I am mentally too weak to shriek in shock, although I needed to. Petra's heart and lung? Is she really dead? I am trying to process all this, but it doesn't compute. I fall asleep again.

I wake up and this time remember everything they previously told me. They must be monitoring my vital signs because almost immediately someone shows up. I have my eyes closed but I am awake.

"How are you feeling, Spinner?" someone asks.

I must be getting better because I am feeling really bad. I am hurting somewhere. Everywhere. Petra is on my mind.

"Why did she die?" I manage to mumble a question.

"Thank God, you're talking! Who, Petra? The medication you brought came too late," I hear the answer. "It had to be tested. We know that it works but it's not without side effects, severe ones. We are working on a version that would eliminate or at least lessen side effects. Many infected women died. The germs are luckily not spreading rapidly, and we have no new cases."

What the hell. Dr. Montenegro! What about Dr. Montenegro? I remember my last conversation with this peculiar character. He said he was going to stop the outbreak because it happened in the future, and I somehow saw it. Why he didn't stop this from happening?

"I need to see Dr. Montenegro," I say quietly, feeling awful.

"Who?" person in the room asks.

"Dr. Montenegro," I repeat. "The hippie doctor who I spoke last with – before my accident?"

The person paused. "Sorry, we have no hippie doctor or any other persons by that name here. You must have mixed this up in your mind or something."

I feel a wave of emotions passing through my body. I am awakened. It's a rude awakening.

"He was supposed to keep any of this from happening," I say trying to stay calm. "What's happening now isn't right. I shouldn't be here; this is a version of reality Dr. Montenegro was supposed to change. He was going to take away the germs before the fanimal mandrill let them loose. I knew the events that didn't occur yet, and because of that, Montenegro was to prevent this from happening. Where is he?"

"I'm sorry, I don't know what you're saying. You must be confused. We have nobody by the name of Dr. Montenegro here. I've worked here for 15 years, you know."

159

This person's words are making me angry, very angry.

"Go to hell!" I try to shout. "Get Mr. Laos, immediately, or I'll kill you!"

That person quickly leaves the room, and I suddenly feel tired, dead tired and black out again.

27

POODLE and BIBLE

I am driving to the Hopkins Motel to collect things left in my room, and to checkout. Unlike before, Main Street is moderately busy, and I need to stop at times to let pedestrians cross the street. I see two kids playing. This is nothing like it was when I first came to Hopkins. Charlie also notices the difference. He points out birds on the ground in the shade of a large tree.

"I'm not familiar with bird names," he says, "but I bet the little ones are house finches, and those black ones are grackles."

I agree and slow down to let a young woman cross the road. She is pushing a stroller with an attached leash, and a small dog at its end. The dog has a curly, light brown coat, and is proudly prancing behind the stroller. Everything is so normal, and I am in a good mood.

"This looks like a poodle," Charlie said. "He's walking as if the world belongs to him."

"Miniature poodle. Smart dog," I agree, following the dog with my eyes.

I park my car in front of the motel lobby and enter. Behind the reception desk are two identical looking young women – the twins, Barbara and Maria. Nobody else is in the lobby. The ladies greet me.

"Let me guess," I say, and point on the girl to my left. "You must be Barbara."

"No," she says, and waives her head.

"I'm Barbara, and she is Maria," the other one says, smiling.

Even though wearing different-colored clothes their faces and hair made them impossible to distinguish.

"How did your visit to Fort Montaus go?" Barbara asks.

"Were you arrested?" Maria adds.

"As you can see, I am here!" I say.

"Did you meet that person you wanted to see there?"

Actually, no. I delivered the remedy for Petra, but it wasn't necessary. There was no disease outbreak, and everything turned hunky-dory. Dr. Montenegro made good on his promise and stopped some bad things from happening. They even showed me around a little bit. However, they wouldn't let me see Petra. They told me she was unavailable, and I could see her at a later time.

"Not really," I answer. "On the one hand I can't see the person I went there for, but on the other, thanks to me, everything changed for everybody. Everything is better now, much better."

"What do you mean?"

"You will think I am crazy, but, for instance, I even saved your life!" I tell Maria, hoping they will not think I am wacky.

"How so?" Maria asks, exchanging looks with her sister.

"You'll not believe me, but you were destined to die in a car accident when you were about six years old, and this didn't happen."

"Funny you should say this," Maria says as her eyes open wide. "I don't really remember this, but our mother told us that once we were playing outside, and I rushed after a ball and a passing car almost ran over me, but swerved and didn't hit me, missing me only by inches. My mother said we both were traumatized from this for some time."

"In one version of reality the car didn't stop in time," I say.

"You are funny, you know?" one of the twins say, and the other one nods, apparently not believing me.

"You don't believe me, right? I don't blame you; I can hardly believe this myself," I say gently.

"Only God can do such a thing, mister," Barbara says.

"And you don't look like God to me," Maria continues and giggles. "Not that we know what God would really look like!"

"You're right – I am not God. But speaking of God, the Bible in my room…"

"Ah, the Bible," she chuckles. "You want to know who blacked out sections of it."

"It was our mother," Maria says.

"She blacked out everything she disagrees with in the Bible," Barbara confirms.

I knew it!

"Our mother," Maria explains. "She was very religious but didn't take anything for granted. She studied the Bible on her own and went on to take out the elements she didn't like. We were curious, of course, and wondered what she had crossed out, and compared the motel's Bible copy with one from the town library. We memorized some of the sentences mother crossed out, and sometimes when we were arguing with her, we would quote the forbidden parts. As expected, this would make her very angry."

"For example, Genesis 19:8," Barbara starts reciting. "Look, I have two daughters who have never slept with a man. Let me bring them out to you, and you can do what you like with them. But don't do anything to these men, for they have come under the protection of my roof."

Wow. I can imagine that most mothers with two daughters would not be happy with that kind of generosity!

This looks similar to my own mother. She never went so far as censoring the Bible but came close. Her methods were different, and she would constantly try to remind everybody around her that they should live by God's words. And, no matter what I did, she was never satisfied.

I announce I need to get my stuff from my room, and that I would be checking out.

As I approach my room and start turning the key to open the door, a sudden wave of fear and horror overwhelms me. The hairs on my neck rise and I begin to shiver. I slowly turn the knob on the door and begin pushing the door open.

As the door opens about a quarter way in ...

28

BIRTHDAY and MARRIAGE

I am sitting on the corner of the living room sofa with a bottle of beer in my hand, listening to *Working My Way Back to You*, by the Spinners, the group that inspired my mother and grandmother to name me.

> *I'll be working my way back to you, babe*
> *With a burning love inside*
> *Hey, I'm working my way back to you, babe*
> *And the happiness that died.*

I hadn't heard the song in a long time, and I am actually enjoying listening to it.

I am at my mother's birthday bash. Mother was in touch with Petra, and Petra was the one who talked me into attending. Mother declined revealing her age, only saying that it was a round number, and she would rather not disclose it.

The party is crowded with unknown and known people. There

are ladies from my mother's church, couples from her neighborhood and other friends. They were all introduced to me and I instantly forgot their names. But it was the people known to me who were at the party that shook me to my core.

The song I am currently listening to is coming out of a speaker connected to a good, old turntable, and the DJ is my father. This was my first big surprise of the evening. Upon our arrival I was almost blown away when a man showed up from my mother's bedroom and introduced himself as my father. I learned that he recently moved from Latvia back to the U.S. My mother was the only person he knew here, and she invited him to her house. Yes, Mom's passion for him never completely died. I didn't recognize him; as I was very young the last time I saw him in person. All I remember was that he didn't want to marry my mother and how hurtful that was for her. I had to force myself not to openly display my hostility toward him. Besides, his asymmetrical appearance, caused by missing an arm, was unpleasant to observe.

"If he is good enough for your mother to take him back, that should be good enough for you," Charlie suggested.

Agreed. I tried to reciprocate the friendliness he expressed toward me, which appeared genuine.

"You and I should get together sometime. I have some ideas and maybe we could do some business together," he said.

That was the end of our conversation for the evening as he was busy making sure to keep the party spirit up with oldies.

But this wasn't all. A bigger surprise came while we were already snacking and making small talk. There was another ring at the door. It was none other than Mr. Laos. He was accompanied by Walter, Max and Lutz himself – a fanimal mandrill. The colorful monkey with long canines walking around unrestrained caused most guests and my parents to almost freak out.

"No need to worry, people!" Max exclaimed. "This is a perfectly harmless and well-behaved monkey. I know, it's hard to believe, but

166

he is my brother."

The party attendees nervously laughed and expressed their awe through the buzz but tried to keep their distance from this strange guest. One person even found the courage to make a joke. "Hey, I can see the resemblance!" The fact that the guests were older people and most of them already had a glass or two of alcohol helped, and nobody tried to escape in horror by jumping out the window. Max added that Lutz was given a drug that was supposed to calm him down and prevent any outburst of anger.

Petra ignored Mr. Laos but showed great interest in Lutz. The two of them soon went to corner quietly conversing. I don't know if other guests realized that the mandrill was actually talking with Petra.

Walter greeted me and introduced me to Max, who acted as if he didn't know me. Mr. Laos also approached me.

"Nice to see you, Mr. Spinner!" he started. "I came here because Petra told me that you were coming to this party. I'd like to personally thank you. What you told Dr. Montenegro allowed us to prevent a disaster. If it had happened, it would be me who would be ultimately blamed for causing it. Dr. Montenegro contacted me and reported everything about the conversation you had. We immediately went to Max and together convinced Lutz to peacefully surrender the box with the vials and germs. Lutz softened up after we told him that his ex, Tilly, would also pay with her life if the events unfold the way you described them. Despite his animosity toward women, he still has feelings for Tilly. This saved many lives, including my daughter's, Petra's and Lydia's. I'll be forever indebted to you for this."

Finally, I received some praises and expressions of gratitude for what I had done. I admit, it made me feel good, very good. I accepted the hand that Mr. Laos offered, and we had a firm, friendly handshake.

Petra also came to me, all excited. "Lutz has no remorse for killing himself and being fused with a mandrill," she said. "I can't tell you how interesting it is to hear about his experience in having the body and organs of a mandrill, and his own human brain which was also connected to the mandrill's."

This was not the last surprise from Petra. She said that she previously spoke with my mother, and they were talking marriage. My mother was concerned that Petra and I lived outside wedlock and was comparing this with her own experience when she was in a relationship with my father and not being married. Petra continued and told me that she said to my mother 'why not.' She and I were living together as a couple, and it looked like we were committed to each other, so – why not. This shocked me. I was under the impression Petra wouldn't even think about it, and to get married with a little crook like myself was unacceptable to her. As a person working for the police department this was an obstacle I thought she could never overcome.

So, I am sitting on the corner of the living room sofa, regurgitating what just happened. I got a praise from Mr. Laos, and Petra is now talking marriage. My dad is back in town, and everybody is alive, including the fanimal Lutz. Life is good.

Next, my mother comes to me, obviously in a good mood. I didn't hear her talking religion the entire evening.

"It looks your father and I will finally get married," she says, and sits next to me. "It would be nice if we could celebrate two weddings on the same day."

I admit the prospect of marrying Petra makes me feel good. I am not even jealous of Mr. Laos who I know would make a pass at Petra if the opportunity presented itself. But she chose me over an older than me, but still good-looking billionaire.

"Go tell your grandmother the news," my mother says, and it was my turn to freak out. My grandmother is still alive? This is all so confusing. I don't know what time it is, and what is real and what is not.

I get up and go to grandma's bedroom. I find her resting in bed, frail and sleeping.

"Hi grandma, it's Spinner," I say and put my hand in hers. Her hand is cold, and she is squeezing it – which I interpret as a sign that she hears me.

I say that I am probably getting married to my girlfriend Petra, and we are likely to be married on the same day my mother and father will finally get married. I also say that I have the necklace and the coins, and that I made my girlfriend, Petra, the designated keeper of the necklace. I don't forget to tell grandma that she was forgiven for what she did when she threw the necklace on her husband's lover, because it was justified.

Grandma remains asleep as I talk to her, but she is squeezing my hand firmer and I see a smile on her white face. I interpret this as her approval for everything I said.

I lean over my grandma's face and give her a kiss on the cheek. Her smile is still there. I say goodbye and feel sad, for I know this is the last time I will see her alive. I know she is going to die happy.

I am choked up exiting the room and here comes Charlie's voice. He was quiet most of the evening.

"Spinner," he says, "wake up, we need to talk."

29

DREAMS and FANTASIES

I am again hanging between nothing and nowhere. I don't feel pain, and suddenly I can't see. Thankfully, Charlie is still with me, although his 'we need to talk' sentence caused me to respond with an 'uh–oh' thought. I am grateful that he didn't leave me, but thinking, what the hell is wrong now?

"You have been in and out of it, man," Charlie starts, "and I don't know if you heard everything that it was said around you. I'd like to confirm that you know what is going on, because I'm not sure I do."

I vaguely remember that I tried to leave the military base with my car. I hit some kind of barrier that unexpectedly blocked the road. I remember hearing somebody say that I was in a coma. I also remember, even more vividly, that I left the base and went back to my motel and had a chat with both twins sisters.

"Your life is still hanging by a thread," Charlie continues. "They operated on you three times. At this point they can't tell if you make it, whether you will be able to walk again."

Wow, that bad, huh? This could explain why I feel no pain. The nerves connecting my head to my body must be pretty messed up, if not completely severed. No, they can't be totally cut off because if they were, the people trying to put me together would know that. They would already say I was a quadriplegic for life. But Charlie said they are not sure. Gee, it looks like I am at least still capable of some reasoning.

"Where am I, and what is going on?" I ask, expecting Charlie to shed more light on all this.

"You are in a hospital which is part of the Fort Montaus military base, and near where the Duke of Prunes medical facilities were relocated to. Frankly, I worry if you are of sound mind. If you don't mind, I'd like to ask you a few questions."

What the hell is Charlie talking about? Of course, I am of sound mind. Even more than that. I have some kind of superpower which allowed me to witness some future events. Thanks to that, a major catastrophe had been avoided. It saved life of Petra, Elizabeth, Lydia, even Lutz's, and others, and now this Bozo is questioning my sanity? I am becoming frustrated.

"Ask me," I say. "Ask me whatever you'd like. What do you want to know?"

"All right. I'd like to know who in the world is this Dr. Montenegro?" Charlie asks.

I can't believe what I hear. My alter ego is now aligning with idiots who keep covering up their own screwups? I am really angry, thinking Charlie is full of shit. If he doesn't know who Dr. Montenegro is, how come he knows his name?

"Charlie, get a hold of yourself," I say. "If you don't know who Dr. Montenegro is, how the hell do you know his name?"

"A few days ago, when you briefly came out of a coma, you demanded to see Dr. Montenegro. Nobody knew who you were talking about, including myself," Charlie explained using his female voice, which means he is also becoming upset.

Somehow, I am able to keep my composure. Generally, I would feel like exploding in situations like this one.

"Charlie, after that military guy interviewed me and walked out with the medication I brought in, Dr. Montenegro, who looked like a hippie, showed up. Don't you remember that? We figured out that the events at the Chicago zoo, with me present, hadn't yet occurred. On that basis he thought that bad things pending could be prevented. And obviously they were avoided. Damn it, Charlie, weren't you there when I had this meeting with Dr. Montenegro?"

"Of course, I was there – I am and was with you all the time. This is what worries me, because there was no Dr. Montenegro and your meeting with that person never happened. Remember, I only know what you see and hear, and I can't read your thoughts."

What the hell? WHAT THE BLOODY HELL!? Here we go again!

"Then what the hell did I do when the first guy left the room with the remedy? Was I taking a siesta?" I ask angrily.

"Well, you only sat there staring at the wall, deeply immersed into your thoughts. I didn't want to disturb you. Then the siren went off, and you jumped from your chair, ran to the exit and knocked down the soldier who showed up at the door announcing that Major Clandon was dead. You asked me for directions, and I helped you back to your car. You jumped in it and drove off like a maniac. When you came close to the gate, a metal plate popped up fast from the ground and the car slammed into it, probably going over 60 miles per hour."

It is hard to accept what Charlie just said, but deep down I suspect he is telling the truth. Yes, I am confused, and I am apparently going nuts.

"What about my mother's birthday party yesterday? Are you saying that everything that happened there didn't happen?" I ask.

"Right," Charlie says. "I know nothing about this party. The last time you saw your mother was on the day Petra dumped you, your grandmother passed away, and your mother kicked you out of the house."

"And I never saw my father at the party and in the library, either?" I ask, while the facts I hear are burning into my mind.

"No," Charlie says. "Afraid not."

"What about the twins in that motel? And their mother who censored the Bible?"

"If it did happen, I would know about it, Spinner," Charlie says. "You hit that metal plate really hard, and never made it back to the motel."

"What about my visit to the zoo with Petra?" I insist. "She later touched the necklace, but I saved her because I pronounced her a designated keeper of it. That also didn't happen?"

"Not at all," Charlie says. "Petra is dead, Spinner. Your remedy came in too late. You imagined all this in your attempt to create a better reality. You must have been dreaming, or hallucinating. I am very sorry. I really am."

I am crushed. Yes, I am insane. I am certain I will be spending the rest of my life in an institution.

"So, I am totally crazy."

"Not necessarily. You've suffered a near fatal trauma during times when several bad events took place. Your mind was overloaded, first with negative reality, and then with the people you were dealing with who stubbornly kept covering up whatever they screwed up. The whole situation with Lutz, the fire, the viruses, Tilly's death, Keith's robbing you, plus everything else what happened. This all on top that Petra leaving you, your grandmother dying, and your mother kicking you out of her house. No wonder you felt alone, and you simply couldn't take it anymore. You figured out the positive outcome in your mind and created Dr. Montenegro to help you find relief and a solution. You made him convince you that the real events that took place in Chicago, didn't happen yet. With parallel realities and all this additional mumbo-jumbo, you made it possible to avoid and correct whatever the grim reality brought you. You fantasized, dreamed, and in your imagination created a different reality, kinder, more positive and attractive than the real one. No, Spinner, I don't think you are a complete nutcase, you just tried to find a way to escape something you coped with and couldn't tolerate any longer."

As Charlie is telling me all this, everything is coming into place. I trust every word he said. I accept I can't escape the real world. I am not crazy, and I wish I were. There is no happy ending. Petra is dead, and I came out of this not as hero but a cripple.

"I need to accept that Petra is dead, and that I might never walk again," I say bitterly. "Basically, I am sane, but totally destroyed."

"At least you have Petra's heart and lung. If it weren't for that, you would be dead, and I along with you. I wish I had better news for you. But there is even more on the plate for you. It will be up to Mr. Laos to tell you. I know this will anger you even more but trust me – every cloud has a silver lining, even this one."

I don't care to process what Charlie is saying, nor am I taking him seriously. After what I just heard, I can't imagine what else could possibly be so outrageous that it could be worse than the revelations I just learned.

As usual, it will turn out that I am wrong again.

30

BODY and CONTROL

"Mr. Spinner, can you hear me?" I hear Mr. Laos' characteristic voice. I recognize his distinctive way of addressing me. I try to open my eyes, but they remain shut. Nevertheless, I can hear him well. Yes, I hear you, I try to say, but words are not coming out of my mouth. I attempt to nod and move, but nothing happens. Obviously, I am paralyzed. At least I feel no pain. It is like being submerged in a gelatin of a kind that matched my own body temperature and consistency that makes me fully blended with my surroundings. I am floating in space without gravity to tell me what is up and what is down.

"Anyway, I'm very much looking forward to hearing what you'll have to say, Mr. Spinner," Mr. Laos continues. "I sincerely hope you will recover. Let me now quickly give you the latest update. The medication you brought to the base led us to come up with a remedy against this nasty infection which is more effective than Mr. Lutz's original preparation. So far, we know of no side effects, and the disease is now completely under control. Unfortunately, it came too late for my lovely Elizabeth. My daughter was everything I ever truly cared for and losing her was like someone ripped my heart out of my body. Miss Petra and Lydia also didn't make it. The pain and guilt I personally have because of this I can't even begin to describe. I also regret my foolish fling with Miss Petra. Our short relationship didn't bring happiness to anybody. If this is of any consolation for you, Miss Petra insisted she keep working here as Alex's guardian, and to be a liaison between our research center and 3ACS fanatics. She refused to quit and accompany me on my trips, and our affair was short-lived. I tell you, her rejection to change her lifestyle despite everything I offered was a blow to my self-esteem. I believe that from the beginning she regretted leaving you. Our efforts to stop that lunatic Lutz from doing what he did created such a stressful situation for all of us and made us all vulnerable. Our actions were based on emotional impulses, and not on rational reasoning. You were actually the only one who came out shining because of how you handled yourself. You tried to save Lutz, and almost died in the process. You also tried to save others, including Miss Petra, by taking the medication to Fort Montaus. You've done this despite the fact that you and Miss Petra were no longer together. This was a nice and selfless gesture from you. My analysis of your psychological profile was correct. Despite being involved in unlawful activities in the past, you retained certain moral characteristics I find commendable. I'd like you to know that I recognize and appreciate this. The disease caused by Lutz's bacteria attacked only women's wombs but left many of their other organs intact. This is how Miss Petra's heart and lung continue living in you, as a transplant. Before they died, all three women requested that their brains be used for experimental fusion with other organisms. They wanted to contribute to scientific medical research and extend their lives within their respective animals. We honored their wishes. My Elizabeth is fused with a young chimpanzee, your Miss Petra with a female German Shepherd and Lydia with a juvenile alpaca. All three fanimals are doing well. Alex is gone, but he didn't die in vain. Thanks to him we found a way to significantly delay, if not completely prevent fused organisms rejecting each other's organs. I hope these three fanimals will remain living for the entire natural life span of the individual animals the ladies are fused with."

Mr. Laos stops talking and I try to open my eyes again. I just want to say, 'you bastard,' but my mouth remains shut and I am helpless. I realize I should have a strong emotional reaction to what I just heard, but I remain unresponsive. I must have been messed up pretty badly.

"You were seriously injured, Mr. Spinner," Mr. Laos changes the subject. "The chance of your surviving the accident was slim, and our surgical teams did several delicate surgeries and procedures in efforts to keep you alive and to put you together. Because of your fluid physical condition my medical research team proposed that an experiment is done on you. I thought about this very hard, and at the end I approved. This was to be a test that could potentially help many patients suffering mental illness. What's been done, Mr. Spinner, was some rewiring of certain areas within your brain. This manipulation is supposed to affect the physical section of your brain where your alter ego presumably resides. Essentially, the idea was to switch between your and Charlie's psyches. This was never done before. If this is successful it will pave the way for medical advances that could further make possible treating some mental illness for which we still have no proper cure yet. For you personally, you might have become Charlie's alter ego and Charlie is possibly now in control of your body."

Mr. Laos stops talking for a second, while the meaning of his words slowly sinks into me. He continues. "At this point we still don't know if this switching really took place. This is why I am eager to talk to you. If this worked, I am actually talking to Charlie right now, while you, Mr. Spinner, are in the background as his alter ego. I am anticipating that you recover and will be able to communicate.

Then we will know if the switch was done successfully. Now you are updated, Mr. Spinner. I'll be checking up on you again tomorrow."

I hear what was being said but I can't believe it. Did I really become my own alter ego? Is Charlie now basking in my body and controlling its functions? Is this why I can't say what I want to say and open my eyes per my own will? And why I can't feel any parts of me, not even pain? Is this why this sneak Charlie wasn't communicating with me lately? I think we are alone in the room, and I start talking.

"Charlie, are you here?" I ask but my mouth doesn't open.

"Yes, I am here," Charlie says through my own mouth. He opens my eyes and I can see now that Mr. Laos is still in the room.

"Spinner heard everything what you said, Mr. Laos," my mouth spit out the words, but it was Charlie who said it.

"If you're not pulling my leg, this is fantastic!" Mr. Laos exclaims excitingly.

"This is bullshit!" I say in my own angry female voice, but my mouth doesn't open.

"He said 'this is bullshit,'" Charlie says through my mouth.

Mr. Laos is ecstatic. "This is fantastic!" he repeats. "Am I really talking to Charlie?"

"Yes, this is Charlie," Charlie says.

"Wait until I tell my team that their experiment was a total success!"

And Mr. Laos quickly leaves the room. I am mildly devastated as my emotions are not real – I only remember them. All I know is that I am screwed up again. I hate Charlie. He must be enjoying taking over my physical body and senses. I am reduced to what he hears and sees, and even this only at his mercy. Although none of this happened due to his own doing, I can't stop blaming him for the situation. My body is stolen, and I am the solitary confinement prisoner within it. Charlie is now in charge. I like to think maybe it's good that my body is in such a bad shape. Maybe I will die soon, and he will not be able to enjoy the benefits of what's left of my body.

"Are you happy now?" I message him.

"I didn't ask for this to happen, Spinner," he says. "Your body – my body now, is in poor condition, and we might not make it. What I got is not exactly a treasure, you know. If you want to know, I am in pain. Every bone I have hurts, and I am very weak. I don't know if I like the trade. If you didn't damage yourself like you did, maybe I would feel differently, but right now I am equally pissed at you, as you are at me."

Blah-blah, Charlie was always a complainer. But perhaps this time he is right. If we don't die, a long physical therapy is ahead. Pain and suffering. Long term inability to enjoy running, even walking. Truth to the matter, I didn't enjoy these things even before my accident. And he might be spending the rest of the life in a wheelchair. He might even have to have assistance wiping his ass. Maybe I am unfair to him. Maybe I am lucky to be avoiding all this. I will only witness this from the margins, without being directly affected in this misery. And maybe thoughts like these are a product of my attempt to turn life's lemons into lemonade. What do I know?

Well, maybe this is what I deserve. If I didn't awaken this damn alter ego in me none of this would happen. Charlie once told me to stay vertical, and I did. Too bad, this is no longer possible.

This is no happy ending for me. And likely, this will not be a happy ending for Charlie either. Happy ending as a figure of speech is nothing but an oxymoron. There are no happy endings. Every ending sucks. And even if something somehow finishes on a happy note, it is not an ending but becomes a new beginning. If our life by any chance does happen to return to normal it will be a new beginning, however not for me, but for my ex-alter ego, Charlie.

More Spinner adventures continue
in upcoming sequel

SPINNER

AND ALL OR NOTHING

—— (1995). *Anticipating China: Thinking Through the Narratives of Chinese and Western Culture.* Albany: State University of New York Press.

—— (1987). *Thinking Through Confucius.* Albany: State University of New York Press.

Hansen, Chad (1992). *A Daoist Theory of Chinese Thought.* Oxford: Oxford University Press.

Henricks, Robert (2000). *Lao Tzu's Tao Te Ching.* New York: Columbia University Press.

—— (1989). *Lao-tzu Te-Tao Ching.* New York: Ballantine.

James, William (2000). *Pragmatism and Other Writings.* Edited by Giles Gunn. New York: Penguin.

Jingmenshi Bowuguan 荆門市博物館 (1998). *Guodian Chumu zhujian* 郭店楚墓竹簡 (The bamboo strip texts from a Chu tomb at Guodian). Beijing: Wenwu chubanshe.

Jullien, François (1995). *The Propensity of Things: Toward a History of Efficacy in China.* Translated by Janet Lloyd. New York: Zone Books.

Karlgren, Bernhard (1975). "Notes on Lao-Tse." *Bulletin of the Museum of Far Eastern Antiquities* 47–48:1–18.

King, Ambrose (1985). "The Individual and Group in Confucianism: A Relational Perspective." In *Individualism and Holism: Studies in Confucian and Taoist Values,* edited by D. Munro. Ann Arbor: University of Michigan Press.

Knoblock, John (1994). *Xunzi: A Translation and Study of the Complete Works.* Vol. III. Stanford: Stanford University Press.

LaFargue, Michael (1998). "Recovering the *Tao-te-ching*'s Original Meaning: Some Remarks on Historical Hermeneutics." In *Lao-tzu and the Tao-te-ching,* edited by Livia Kohn and Michael LaFargue. Albany: State University of New York.

—— (1994). *Tao and Method: A Reasoned Approach to the* Tao Te Ching. Albany: State University of New York Press.

—— (1992). *The Tao of the Tao Te Ching.* Albany: State University of New York Press.

Lau, D. C. (1982). *Chinese Classics: Tao Te Ching.* Hong Kong: Chinese University of Hong Kong Press.

Lau, D. C., and Roger T. Ames (1996). *Sun Pin: The Art of Warfare.* New York: Ballantine.

Legge, James (1891). *The Texts of Taoism*. In *Sacred Books of the East*. Oxford: Oxford University Press.

Li Ling 李零 (1995-6). "An Archeological Study of Taiyi (Grand One) Worship," translated by Donald Harper. *Early Medieval China* 2.

Needham, Joseph (1956). *Science and Civilisation*. Vol. II. Cambridge: Cambridge University Press.

Neville, Robert Cummings (1974). *The Cosmology of Freedom*. New Haven: Yale University Press.

Pang Pu 龐朴 (1998). "Kong-Meng zhi jian—Guodian Chu jian de sixiangshi diwei 孔孟之間—郭店楚簡的思想史地位 (Between Confucius and Mencius—the place in the history of thought of the Chu strips found at Guodian)." *Zhongguo Shehui Kexue* 中國社會科學 (Social Sciences in China) 5:88–95.

Roth, Harold D. (1999). *Original Tao: Inward Training and the Foundations of Taoist Mysticism*. New York: Columbia University Press.

Ryle, Gilbert (1949). *The Concept of Mind*. London: Hutchinson.

Schaberg, David (1999). "Song and the Historical Imagination in Early China." *Harvard Journal of Asiatic Studies* 59:2.

Sivin, Nathan (1995). *Medicine, Philosophy and Religion in Ancient China: Researches and Reflections* (Aldershot, HANTS: Variorum, 1995).

Tang Junyi 唐君毅 (1988). "Zhongguo zhexue zhong ziranyuzhouguan zhi tezhi 中國哲學中自然宇宙觀之特質 (The distinctive features of natural cosmology in Chinese philosophy)." In *Zhongxi zhexue sixiang zhi bijiao lunwenji* 中西哲學思想之比較論文集 (Collected essays on the comparison between Chinese and Western philosophical thought). Taipei: Xuesheng shuju.

Tredennick, Hugh, and Harold Tarrant (1993). *Plato: The Last Days of Socrates*. London: Penguin Books.

Waley, Arthur (1934). *The Way and Its Power: A Study of the Tao Te Ching and Its Place in Chinese Thought*. London: Allen and Unwin.

Wang Hui 王暉 (2000). *Shang Zhou wenhua bijiao yanjiu* 商周文化比較研究 (A comparative study of Shang and Zhou cultures). Beijing: Renmin chubanshe.

Watson, Burton (trans.). (1968). *The Complete Works of Chuang Tzu*. New York: Columbia University Press.

Whitehead, A. N. (1978). *Process and Reality* (corrected edition). Edited by D. Griffin and D. Sherburne. New York: The Free Press.

——— (1926, rep. 1996). *Religion in the Making.* New York: Macmillan. Reprinted by Fordham University Press, New York.

Wu Yi 吳怡 (2001). *Xinyi Laozi jieyi* 新譯老子解義 (A new translation of the *Laozi* with commentary). Taipei: Sanmin shuju.

Xiong Shili 熊十力 (1977). *Mingxinpian* 明心篇 (An essay on illuminating the mind). Taibei: Xuesheng shuju.

Zhang Dongsun 張東蓀 (1995). *Zhishi yu wenhua: Zhang Dongsun wenhua lunzhu jiyao* 知識與文化：張東蓀文化論著輯要 (Knowledge and culture: The essential writings on culture by Zhang Dongsun). Edited by Zhang Yaonan 張耀南. Beijing: Zhongguo guangbo dianshi chubanshe.

About the Authors

ROGER T. AMES is a professor of Chinese philosophy at the University of Hawai'i. He is also editor of the journal *Philosophy East and West*. He is the author of several interpretive studies of classical Confucianism, including *Thinking Through Confucius* (with David L. Hall). His translation of *Sun-tzu: The Art of Warfare* is recognized as a landmark of contemporary Chinese military and philosophical studies and his translation of *The Analects of Confucius* (with Henry Rosemont Jr.) has become a popular classroom text.

DAVID L. HALL was a professor of philosophy at the University of Texas at El Paso. His early research on A. N. Whitehead and American philosophy led him to rethink our understanding of both Daoism and classical Greek philosophy, and resulted in the publication of *The Uncertain Phoenix* and *Eros and Irony*. In addition to the interpretive studies of classical Chinese philosophy, he continued to publish in American philosophy with *Richard Rorty: Prophet and Poet of the New Pragmatism*.